VANESSA'S CHOICE

Rowdy Rooksy

RowdyGunnshy Productions

"For every reader who has ever felt like they had to choose - this one's for you. May you always have the courage to break the rules and follow your heart."

~ Rowdy

AUTHOR'S NOTE

Writing Vanessa's story wasn't an option. lol! When I tell ya'll this character was running wild in my head day and night, I mean that. I had to tell her story.

Vanessa is a supporting character from my *Thorns And Gloves* novel. That is where we got a glimpse into her life, and we met the two MMCs in this story, Gage and Vince for the first time. Vanessa was funny, wild and sexy in that story. And the way she cut for her bestie, Gabby, in that story was so on point.

Even though this story is a spinoff from *Thorns And Gloves*, it is a standalone. I do, however, encourage you to read Thorns And Gloves if you haven't. It's a great love story.

TRIGGER WARNINGS

This is a love story but there are some elements that may not jive with you. Check the triggers below. Your mental health is important to me, so if any of the items listed below affect you in a negative way, please don't proceed with this story.

Triggers
 * Explicit Sexual Content
 * Violence (MMC is a boxer)
 * Strong Language
 * BDSM Elements
 * Polyamourous Relationship
 * Scenes of Emotional Conflict
 * Dicussion of Death of Parents

VANESSA'S
CHOICE

PLAYLIST ⌄

▶ **Can't Take My Eyes Off You**
Lauryn Hill   03.41

▶ **Girls Need Love**
Summer Walker   02.21

▶ **Sexy Love**
Ne-Yo   03.41

▶ **Moment of Your Life**
Brent Faiyz feat. Coco Jones   03.15

▶ **ICU**
Coco Jones   04.02

▶ **The Heart Wants What It Wants**   03.47
Selena Gomez

▶ **Un-thinkable (I'm Ready)**
Alicia Keys   04.09

▶ **3Way**
Teyana Taylor   03.24

▶ **More Than Enough**
Alina Braz   02.31

CONTENTS

CHAPTER ONE

VANESSA

The hum of the city faded into the background as I flitted around the room, putting the final touches on what I hoped would be the perfect engagement party. This wasn't just any party; it was for Gabby and Griff. Gabby, my girl, my bestie, my ride-or-die, and Griff, the man who'd last year, turned her world—and, inadvertently, mine —upside down in the worst and ultimately the best way.

The venue was something out of a magazine, with its high ceilings, sprawling windows that gave way to the twinkling lights of Eastbrook, and elegant decor that screamed chic yet intimate. Each table was adorned with delicate floral arrangements courtesy of my girl Gabby's flower shop, Bloomed in Eastbrook, and soft, ambient music floated through the air, mingling with my favorite scent of lavender and vanilla.

"Vanessa, this place looks amazing! You outdid yourself, child," Momma Gwen's voice, rich with approval, pulled me from my reverie.

I flashed her a grateful smile. "Thanks, Momma Gwen. I wanted everything to be perfect."

And it had to be. This wasn't just about celebrating love; it was a testament to new beginnings, second chances, and the kind of love stories you read about. Gabby and Griff were couple goals. The way Griff loved and supported Gabby was something of fairytales. I'm convinced that man would go to hell and back for my bestie, and I loved that about him. Yeah, this was going to be a great evening. But as I adjusted a slightly crooked napkin for the umpteenth time, my stomach did a nervous flip.

Unlike Gabby, relationships weren't really my thing, so I didn't do them. I mean, I kept a small stable of men that I fucked with, but getting into something serious was just never on my agenda. I mean, it didn't use to be. Now, I'm not so sure. I'd been consistently hooking up with the same two men over the past year, and I'd watched my affection grow for them both in ways I had never imagined. And tonight, they'd both be in attendance.

The two men making me rethink my unattached life - Gage Emerson and Vince Cartwright.

With his easy smile and eyes that always seemed to dance with mischief, Gage breezed into my life seemingly out of nowhere. He showed up a year ago to train for a big fight with Griff, and even though he's not based in Eastbrook, he spent the majority of his time here. He claimed it was because he wanted to keep training with Griff, but

I knew better. He came here to train with Griff, but he's sticking around for me and my magical pum-pum.

And then there's Vince, the epitome of tall, dark and handsome. And if that wasn't enough, he was mad intelligent, and super protective of me. Oh, and the way he looked at me - the man had a gaze so intense it made me feel like the only person in the room.

Both of them had somehow managed to entangle themselves in my thoughts and, dare I say, my heart, in an exhilarating and terrifying way.

I let out a deep breath, trying to shake off the nerves. I needed to focus. This night was about Gabby and Griff, not my confusing, tangled-up feelings.

Guests began to trickle in, laughter and chatter filling the once quiet space. I greeted everyone as they arrived and felt a sense of pride swell in my chest at all the community members who came out to support Gabby and Griff. They'd become pillars in the community, working with the residents to make changes to Eastbrook that benefited everyone.

I timed it so that all the guests would arrive first so that Gabby and Griff could make a grand entrance.

"You good, child?" Momma Gwen asked, pulling me from my thoughts.

I smiled brightly at her. "I'm fine. Just going

through my mental checklist to make sure everything's covered."

Momma Gwen patted my arm supportively. "I'm sure you got everything covered, but if you need my help..."

The rest of Momma Gwen's statement was lost on me as the door opened, revealing Gage's tall frame, followed by Vince's commanding presence. My heart skipped a beat. Of course, they arrived at the same time, looking fine as fuck, and the way they scanned the room until their eyes landed on me made my pulse quicken.

"Okay?" Momma Gwen's voice pulled me back to her.

I had no idea what she'd said, so I replied, "Okay, Momma Gwen."

That seemed to satisfy her because she smiled and moved on to talk to other guests.

I straightened the napkin on the table one more time. I was stalling. I needed to say hi to Gage and Vince, but my nerves were on edge having them in the same place at the same time. I was good at juggling men as long as they were kept apart.

"What up, Dimples?" Gage's voice cut through my thoughts, a smooth blend of warmth and charm. I turned to face him as he made his way to me, my heart fluttering despite my attempts to remain composed. He looked so good. He was dressed to the nines in a blue Brioni suit I knew was tailored because it fit him to a T.

Gage moved close to me, invading my space.

His familiar charm was in full swing, and a flurry of butterflies erupted in my stomach. "Hey, Hercules," I replied, my voice steady despite the inner chaos he always seemed to ignite. Watching him in that perfectly tailored suit, I couldn't help but remember the effortless way he could dismantle my composure with that charming ass smile of his. I caught myself lingering on the memory of his mouth on my body, a dangerous territory I quickly steered away from.

Gage chuckled at his nickname. "Keep playin'. Imma show you just what Hercules can do later."

Shit! There went my panties. That was the thing about Gage. The man had the ability to keep my panties wet. It was a gift and a curse. This push and pull with Gage, this dance between flirtation and something deeper, kept me on edge.

"Calm down, Cujo," I joked, loving how easy it was for us to slip into this playful banter.

"Whatever, shawty. The place looks good," he said, his gaze sweeping the room before settling back on me. "You've outdone yourself, V."

"Thanks. You know I had to make it perfect for our besties," I replied with a toothy grin.

"Yeah. They deserve it. Those two were made for each other," he said.

"It's almost disgusting how perfect they are together," I said and pretended to throw up in disgust.

Gage's smile widened. "You wild, Dimples."

"And you love it," I said, the words coming out

without thought.

Gage leaned in closer, his voice lowering. "I'm definitely partial to it, shawty."

My belly tightened at his nearness- at his words and at the drugging scent of sweet, earthy, warm spice wafting from him, and encircling me. He was wearing Tom Ford Black Orchid cologne—my kryptonite.

I found myself leaning into him. "What else are you partial to?" I flirted.

Before he could answer, a server approached, hesitantly interrupting. "Ms. Davis, there's a question about the champagne order," she said.

"I'll be right there," I told the server, then looked at Gage. "Duty calls," I told him.

"Handle your business, Gorgeous. I'll find you later," he said and placed a soft kiss near the corner of my mouth and I tried hard not to swoon.

"Yeah... okay," was all I could muster. As I walked away, I could feel his gaze on me, sending a shiver down my spine.

After handling the question about the champagne, I took a moment to compose myself before going back into the banquet hall. Gage's ass had me all kinds of rattled. As I entered the banquet hall, Vince made his way toward me. I stopped moving and watched him. He was so damn good-looking with his midnight skin, smoldering hazel eyes, and perfectly built body. I wasn't the only woman in the room watching him stride across the floor. His presence was like a gravity well, drawing in everything around him with his quiet intensity.

"Hey, beautiful," Vince greeted me, his voice deep and resonant. The air between us seemed to crackle. Vince's simple and warm yet intense greeting enveloped me, stirring a different kind of turmoil inside.

"Hey," I replied, my voice softer than I intended. "I'm glad you came."

He offered a small, genuine smile. "Wouldn't miss it. You've done an incredible job. The place looks amazing."

"Thank you. I put a lot into it. You know I had to go big for my girl."

He nodded. "So, I take it you got everything under control. If there's anything I can do, let me know."

I could feel my heart melting. Vince was always looking out for me. Not that Gage didn't. They just had different ways of going about it.

"You right," I told him. "Everything is under control. No help needed."

"Good. Now, how are *you* doing?" He asked.

"Me? I'm good. Don't I look good?" I goaded him.

"You always look good, Vanessa. You know that. And you also know I have to ask about you. Your lil ass be on the move so much I gotta check in and make sure you taking care of you," Vince said, his caramel eyes assessing.

He wasn't wrong. I tended to be a woman on the go, and sometimes that meant neglecting my needs. I appreciated that he was always looking out. His question about my welfare wasn't just a formality but a testament to how he always seemed to see beyond my facade. The way he looked out for me, ensuring I wasn't neglecting myself amidst my hectic life, was comforting and unnerving. And even though I brushed off his offer for help, I was acutely aware of the contradiction within me - the desire for his care and the fear of what it meant.

"Is that your cell buzzing?" Vince asked.

"Huh?" I looked down at my phone. It was a text from Gabby: *"We're parking. Be inside in less than 5."*

"Shit! They're here," I said. "I need to get everyone near the entrance for when they come in. We'll chat later." I told Vince as I started walking away. Oddly, I felt a strange sense of loss at leaving him. I shook my head slightly, attempting to free myself of his hold.

I quickly moved around the room, letting the guests know that Gabby and Griff were there and to focus on the door so we could give them a very loud, very warm welcome to their engagement party.

As the guests turned their attention to the door, I couldn't help but glance back at Vince and Gage, standing on opposite sides of the room, yet both watching me intently. My entire body heated, and I quickly looked away.

As I made my way to the door, the room's energy instantly elevated. The crowd turned expectantly towards the door just as Gabby and Griff walked in, hand in hand. Applause and cheers erupted, filling the room with a joyous noise.

I rushed over to them, wrapping Gabby in a tight hug. "Congrats, bestie!" I exclaimed, feeling a rush of affection and pride for my best friend and her fiancé.

"Thanks, boo," Gabby replied. Her happiness was infectious, and her smile was brighter than I'd ever seen it. And Griff, he looked at her like she was his entire world.

I untangled myself from Gabby and accosted Griff, throwing my arms around his neck and hugging him tightly. "Congrats, brother-in-law."

Griff chuckled as he hugged me back. "Thanks, Vanessa. The place looks great."

I pulled back from the hug and pursed my lips at him. "Uh, duh! Would you expect anything less from ya girl?"

Griff just smiled and shook his head.

"Well, come on in. This is your party. Everyone is here to celebrate you. Mingle. Have some drinks. Dinner will be served in about twenty minutes."

At the bridal party table, I was seated next to Gage, the deliberate distance I'd put between Vince and me across the room doing little to calm my racing heart. I was playing with fire, and I knew it.

Gage, as always, was a master of charm, his playful banter laced with an undercurrent of desire. He leaned in close, his voice a low rumble. "Keep licking that fork like that and I'mma toss your sexy ass on this table and give everybody up in here a show," he teased, his gaze intense yet playful, making my skin tingle and my pussy thump with anticipation.

I squeezed my thighs together, trying to find relief.

"That pussy wet, ain't it?" He continued to tease me.

"No idea what you're talking about, you filthy, filthy boy," I managed to say, trying to sound nonchalant. But it was getting harder to keep up the facade, especially when Gage's hand found its way to my thigh under the table. His fingers trailed up my skin, hidden from view but oh so daring in their exploration.

"Okay. Keep telling yourself that. I know better," Gage whispered as he slid a hand along my thigh, slowly dragging my dress up until my thigh was bare.

I inhaled sharply at the feel of his hands on my skin and completely stopped breathing when he pried said hand between my thighs and skimmed his fingers along my panties. Not one breath was expelled as he dipped a finger beneath the fabric and swiped between my folds.

"Soaked. Just like I said," Gage murmured against my ear, his finger sliding with ease along my slickness. The audacity of his actions, right here in the midst of the party, was both nerve-wracking and hot as fuck.

I watched, heart pounding, as he brought said

finger to his mouth and sucked all my juices from it.

Shit!

Such a brazen move, but hell, that was Gage. The man really was always down to get it in anywhere. He was a freak, and I loved that about him. What he was doing now, at this table, was a promise, a tease, and a challenge all rolled into one. Had it not been my bestie's engagement party, I would have pulled Gage into the nearest closet or bathroom, and that would be all she wrote.

CHAPTER TWO

VANESSA

Laughter and music from the engagement party filled the air. I moved among the guests, ensuring everyone had a good time, yet my mind was elsewhere. The night had taken an unexpected turn, leaving me with a whirlwind of emotions that I struggled to contain.

I watched from a distance as Gage mingled with guests, his laughter booming above the music. His eyes occasionally found mine, and every time, a jolt of electricity shot through me. But it was Vince's presence that had truly unsettled me tonight. He stood near the bar, his deep brown skin glowing under the soft lights, his gaze intense and thoughtful.

As the slow melody of a romantic song began to play, Vince approached me, extending his hand with a gentle smile. "Dance with me?" he asked, his voice a resonant hum that sent shivers down my spine.

I hesitated for a moment, aware of Gage's eyes on us, but the sincerity in Vince's eyes drew me in. I placed my hand in his, and he led me to the dance floor. As we swayed to the music, I could feel the warmth of his body, and the strength in his arms as he held me close. His touch was tender yet protective, enveloping me in a sense of safety and desire.

"God, you feel good," Vince murmured, his lips brushing against my ear.

I leaned into him, my heart racing. "So do you," I whispered back, my voice barely audible over the music.

As the song continued, I found myself lost in the moment, the rest of the world fading away. It was just Vince and me, moving together in perfect harmony. But then, out of the corner of my eye, I saw Gage watching us, his expression unreadable.

The song ended, and Vince released me slowly, his eyes locking onto mine with an intensity that left me breathless. "Can I see you later?" he asked softly.

I wanted to see him. I really did, but I was having so many conflicting emotions right now that it was best for me to go home, sleep these feelings off, and try again tomorrow. "You know I'd love that but I'm already pretty beat from everything I had to do today. I think it's best I go home and get a good night's sleep. But, we can link up tomorrow," I told him.

Disappointment flashed in his hazel eyes, but it was gone as soon as it appeared. "Yeah. Of course. I'm sure you ran yourself ragged putting this thing together. Get some rest tonight, love." Vince said. He shoved his hands in his pockets. "I'mma go grab a drink. You want one?"

"Nah. I'm good. But, thanks. I'm actually going to go check on Gabby," I replied.

"Bet. Maybe I'll hit you up for another dance later," he said, then ran his thumb along my jawline before heading off to find a server.

My nipples tingled, and my mind raced as I watched him walk away. What the hell was he doing to me? Hell, what were both of these men doing to me? Had my insides all jumbled and shit.

"Hey, girlie," Gabby sang as she walked up.

I tore my gaze from Vince and focused on her. "Hey, girl," I said.

Gabby's eyes narrowed as she looked at me. "Follow me," she ordered and started walking.

I didn't even question her. I just followed her, grateful for the chance to step away and gather my thoughts. Who better to do that with than my bestie?

She led me to an empty corner in the back of the room. "You good?" she asked, her eyes filled with concern.

I sighed, the weight of my emotions pressing down on me. "Honestly, bestie, I don't know. Things are getting a little... complicated."

Gabby's brows knit together as she looked at me. "Complicated? The party?"

I shook my head. "Not the party. My damn love life."

She gave an exaggerated nod. "Oh."

"Yeah. You know your girl's a G, but juggling two

men who run in the same circles ain't easy."

Gabby's gaze was sympathetic, her hand reaching out to squeeze mine. "I bet. I don't know how you do it. I could never."

"I don't recommend it, but then again, here we are," I said with a chuckle.

"Why don't you just stop seeing one of them," Gabby suggested.

I shook my head. "If it were only that simple."

Her eyes narrowed. "Isn't it, though? Just pick the one you like the most. They're big boys. They can handle it."

"Oh, I know. That's not the issue." I paused to swallow the lump that had lodged in my throat. "The issue is that I actually... kind of... sort of... really like them both equally."

"Well, that's a problem." Gabby deadpanned.

"Thank you, Captain Obvious," I quipped, and Gabby swatted my shoulder.

"Don't be bitchy because your ass done fell for two guys," she clapped back and my jaw dropped.

"I have not fallen for two men," I said incredulously.

"Yeah, okay. Well, I tell you what. We not gon' resolve this tonight, so I say you steer clear of both of them for the rest of the party. Hang with me. We'll drink, dance, and enjoy the rest of the party together."

"I can do that," I said, slipping my arm around hers. "Let's start with a shot."

Gabby's face scrunched. "Why did I know you

were going to say that? Shots, V? Really? I don't-"

I cut her off. "Nah, lil sis, it was your idea to drink and party to keep my mind off my men, so we doing shots."

Gabby blew out a breath and rolled her eyes in the most dramatic fashion ever. "Fine. Let's go."

We made our way to the bar that was set up across the room and downed a few shots. For the rest of the evening, I did my best to focus on the party and avoid any further interactions with Gage and Vince. They both seemed to peep my need for space and stayed away while keeping eyes on me from afar.

As the night drew to a close, I played the good party host by thanking the guests for coming, sending folks off with to-go plates, and making sure Gabby and Griff's gifts got loaded into Griff's truck before they left. Now it was just me, and the clean-up crew I'd hired.

As the clean-up crew buzzed around, efficiently restoring order to the venue, I found myself standing alone in the now-quiet space. The echoes of laughter and music had faded, replaced by the soft clatter of dishes and the low murmur of voices.   Clean-up was swift, and I was locking the doors in no time.

The night air was cool as I stepped outside, my heels clicking on the pavement. I paused, closing my eyes and taking in a deep breath. As I opened them and started back toward my car, I noticed Vince's silhouette leaning against my newly purchased Infinity QX50 Luxe.

His tall frame was relaxed against the sleek lines of the car, but his eyes were alert, watching me as I approached. The dim lights in the parking lot cast shadows across his features, enhancing the intensity of his gaze.

"Vince?" I asked, my voice tinged with surprise. "What are you doing?"

He pushed off from the car, standing to his full height. "I wanted to make sure you got to your car safely," he replied, his tone casual but underlined with concern.

I couldn't help but smile, touched by his thoughtfulness. "You didn't have to wait, you know. I'm a big girl."

"I know," he said, stepping closer. "But I wanted to. Besides, it gives me a chance to do this."

Before I could question him, Vince closed the distance between us. His hands gently cupped my face, and he leaned down, his lips meeting mine in a kiss that was gentle at first but grew deeper, more intense. The world around me seemed to fade, leaving only the two of us in this small bubble of time and space.

The kiss was slow, lingering, filled with an emotion that sent shivers down my spine. Vince's lips moved against mine with a tenderness that belied the strength in his arms. I melted into him, my hands resting against his chest, feeling the steady beat of his heart as his tongue swirled around mine.

When he finally pulled back, there was a softness in his eyes that I hadn't seen before. "Drive safe," he whispered, his breath warm against my skin.

I nodded, still dazed from the kiss. Vince opened the car door for me, his movements gentle but assured. He helped me in, fastening the seatbelt around me with a care that was almost tender.

As I started the engine, he closed the door and stepped back, his gaze never leaving mine. I rolled down the window, and he leaned in, placing one last kiss on my forehead. "Text me when you get home," he said, his voice a low rumble.

I drove off into the night, Vince's figure growing smaller in the rearview mirror. His kiss lingered on my lips. The drive home was a blur, my mind replaying every moment of our encounter, the way he looked at me, the feel of his lips on mine. Vince had stirred something deep within me, and I wasn't sure whether to draw closer to him or run.

Pulling into my driveway, the sight of Gage's Bentley Betayga parked there caught me off guard. The night was full of surprises, it seemed. I hadn't expected him to be here, but there he was, unfolding himself from his car with that casual grace of his as I got out of mine.

"Didn't expect to see you here," I said, as I sauntered up to him.

Gage flashed a crooked smile. "Just wanted to make sure you got home safe," he said, his voice laced with a care that warmed me.

I grinned up at him despite the whirlwind of emotions I was already dealing with. "Thanks, Gage. That's sweet. Do you want to come in for a coffee?"

"Hell yeah," he said, eyeing me up and down.

"Come on here, boy," I said, grabbing his hand and pulling him up the driveway.

Inside, the familiar comforts of my home felt grounding after the evening's events. As I busied myself in the kitchen making coffee, Gage leaned against the counter, his presence filling the room.

"I know I told you this already, but you really outdid yourself tonight, V," he said, his tone admiring. "It was a really great party."

I glanced over my shoulder at him, sensing there was more behind his words. "Thanks, Gage. Yeah, it was a successful night. Gabby had a blast, and that's all I wanted." I replied, deliberately keeping my tone light.

Gage's gaze lingered on me, a hint of something more in his eyes. "You looked like you were really enjoying yourself too," he said, his voice carrying an unspoken question.

I had a feeling he was alluding to my dance with Vince, but I chose not to delve into that. Instead, I simply nodded. "It was nice to see everyone let loose. And yes, I really enjoyed myself."

He moved closer, his flirtatious energy unmistakable. "Let me add to your good night," he said, his voice dropping to a huskier tone.

I turned to face him, the tension between us

palpable. I didn't need any more words. Closing the gap, I answered him with a kiss that was both a surrender and a declaration. His response was immediate, his arms wrapping around me as our kiss deepened, igniting a fire that had been simmering all evening.

The coffee and any lingering thoughts of Vince were forgotten as I got lost in the moment. The night's earlier confusion melted away into a passion that was undeniable. In Gage's arms, I found a different kind of safety, one that was thrilling and a little dangerous.

CHAPTER THREE

GAGE

The taste of her was intoxicating. As Vanessa's lips moved against mine, a fire ignited within me, burning away any lingering restraint. My hands roamed over her, memorizing every curve and contour of her perfect body while her soft moans filled the air, stoking the flames of my desire.

I pulled back for a moment, our breaths mingling, our foreheads touching. Her eyes, dark and shining, held mine with an intensity that sent a jolt through me. I never did all this kissing shit with other women I'd been with, but kissing Vanessa - it was like diving into a deep, endless ocean, and I was willingly drowning.

"Vanessa," I whispered, my voice rough with emotion. The way she looked at me then, with that mix of vulnerability and strength, did something to me. It was as if she was peeling back layers I didn't even know I had.

Not sure why, but in that moment, a flash of earlier in the evening sliced through my mind — Vanessa in Vince's arms, dancing slowly, intimately. I had watched from across the room, a glass of cognac forgotten in my hand. The sight of them had ignited a feeling I wasn't accustomed to — a sharp, twisting jealousy. I, Gage Emerson, the man who never envied another man's possession because I never wanted to possess a woman before, felt jealousy.

But it was more than that. It wasn't just the sight of her with another man; it was the realization of how deeply she'd embedded herself under my skin. I had come here tonight, telling myself it was to check on her and ensure she made it home safely. But who was I fooling? I needed to see her, be near her, feel her.

As our lips met again, the kiss deepened, becoming a physical manifestation of all the unspoken words between us. My hands tangled in her thick hair, normally worn naturally; tonight was bone straight, shiny, and soft as shit against my fingers. I pulled her closer as if I could merge her being with mine. There was a desperation in my movements, a need to claim her, to mark her as mine, even though I knew that wasn't what this was. Vanessa wasn't a woman to be claimed by anyone. She was a force, wild and free, and damn, did I admire that about her.

Our bodies moved together with a rhythm that felt as natural as breathing. I lifted her effortlessly, setting her on the edge of the counter, and positioned myself between her thick thighs. The heat between us was palpable, the air charged with electricity.

As I looked down at her, her chest heaving,

lips swollen from our kisses, a realization dawned on me. This wasn't just about physical desire. Somewhere along the way, my feelings for Vanessa had morphed into something deeper, something that scared the hell out of me. She was no longer just a casual fling; she was becoming a necessity, an addiction.

"Lift up," I softly commanded.

She used her hands to lift her bottom off the counter, and I pushed the skirt of her dress up so it bunched at her waist, then I pulled off her panties. I stared at her pussy. Her pretty pussy, so fat and already glistening for me, had my mouth watering. I locked eyes with her as I lowered myself between her thighs and then ran my tongue up her slit.

"Oh. Shit. Gage," she moaned as she stared down at me.

I loved hearing the want and ecstasy in her voice. It made me want to gobble her up, so I did. I swirled my tongue, making circles around her clit before sucking her tight little pearl into my mouth. I pulled, nibbled, and sucked on her clit so good she was squirming and pushing at my head.

I gripped her thighs, holding her in place, and continued to devour her pussy. Licking and slurping her from asshole to clit.

"Ah! G-Gage... please," she begged, and my shit damn near bust through my slacks. I loved hearing her beg for me.

"Mmm. You taste so fucking good, V," I groaned

against her slit.

"Mmm-hmm...thank you, baby, but I need to feel you inside me. Please."

I grinned. I knew she wanted the dick, but I wasn't quite ready to give it to her. I needed her coming all over my tongue first.

I latched onto her clit and sucked as I slipped two fingers into her warm, wet hole. I immediately felt her walls tighten and clench around me. I pulsed my fingers back and forth inside her before twisting my hand and tapping my fingers against her sweet spot.

"Oh! Oh! Shit!" Vanessa cried. "G-Gage! I'm bout to... I'm going to... c-come."

"That's right. Be a good girl and come for Daddy," I coaxed against her soaked pussy.

Vanessa's hips bucked, and she ground down on my hand and mouth. I was greedy as I licked and sucked her clit, ready to taste her sweet honey. I thrust my fingers into her harder, stretching that tight little pussy. Her clit seemed to become more sensitive the harder I thrust. She reached down, grasped my hand, and held it in place, then commenced to fucking herself on my fingers.

I watched her through slitted eyes. Her face was a beautiful mask of pleasure with her eyes half-mast, and her bottom lip caged between her teeth. She was so fucking beautiful. I loved seeing her like this, in the throes of passion. And that was the other thing about me and V, our sex game was next level. I was a dominant fuck, and with all her feistiness, she loved being handled in bed. And I loved that shit.

"Gage, I'm about to come, Daddy," she moaned.

"Mmm-hmm. Come on. Come for me," I commanded as I tapped my fingers against her spot again. This time she froze, her body locking and her head falling back, mouth open as her orgasm hit. Her sweet honey gushed from her center, and I drank it up, slurping and sucking to make sure not a drop was wasted.

I stood, her juices glistening on my mouth and beard, and kissed her. I swept my tongue deep into her mouth, letting her taste herself.

"Mmm," she moaned. "Take me to bed and fuck me, Gage," she whined.

Without a word, I lifted her from the counter, and she wrapped her legs around my waist. I placed soft kisses on her mouth and neck as I walked us to her bedroom.

I set her on her feet and quickly rid her of her dress, then started working on my own clothes. I undressed, keeping my eyes on her as she lay back on the bed, looking like a fucking queen. She was propped up on her elbows, pupils blown with lust, legs open, pussy dripping and waiting to be fucked. My shit was so hard it almost hurt.

I climbed onto the bed, spreading her thick legs as wide as they would go, and settled between her thighs. My dick throbbed as it brushed against her soaking slit.

Vanessa's eyes rolled back at the contact, and

she let out a quiet moan.

"Look at me, Vanessa," I quietly commanded, needing to hold her gaze as I pushed into her.

Vanessa focused her gaze on mine, and I slowly sank every inch of my dick into her until my balls were plastered against her pussy.

Vanessa gasped and clutched at my arms, her hands unable to wrap all the way around my biceps as I started moving, stretching her pussy to accommodate me. We fucked a lot, yet her shit was always so damn tight. I wasn't complaining, though. The shit felt too good.

I stroked in and out of her, giving her slow, deep thrusts for a minute before sitting up in a kneeling position. I gripped her hips and pulled her up so her ass rested on my upper thighs and slid her back and forth along my dick. I fucked her this way, hard and fast, as my thumb rubbed gently over her clit.

"Fuck! So good... feels so good, Daddy," she moaned as her walls shook around me.

Shit! I bit down on my lip to keep from moaning myself. The shit felt so good.

"That pussy quiverin'," I murmured down at her. I stilled so the involuntary motions of her inner walls were easily felt.

Vanessa lifted her hips and started rolling them in a needful motion. "Stop teasing," she breathed out and dug her nails into my flesh. I knew she drew blood, but I didn't care. I loved that shit. How wild she was. It only made me start moving again.

"Say less," I told her and wrapped a hand around her throat and squeezed just enough to make it slightly difficult to breathe, then slammed into her pussy over and over again.

I stayed locked on Vanessa as her pretty face contorted in ecstasy. She was on the verge of sensual insanity, every part of her alive with desire. I eased up on her throat a bit as her orgasm came crashing down. She gasped for air as her walls locked me in, grasping my dick and milking me.

"Shit, V, you bout to make me come," I grunted.

"Mmm... come on, Daddy. Come with me," she coaxed.

I growled and covered her body with mine. I fastened my teeth on the side of her neck, pinning her in place as I pounded her pussy and shot my seed into her. Galaxies exploded before my eyes, and euphoria took over as my cum cascaded inside her, coating her walls.

I pressed little kisses to her neck, face, and mouth before pulling out and going to the bathroom to clean myself up and grab a towel to clean her up.

I let out a small laugh as I walked back into the room to find Vanessa passed the fuck out, arm thrown over her face, legs still spread wide open. I gently cleaned between her legs, tossed the rag into her hamper, and climbed back into bed. I pulled her to me, and she snuggled against my chest.

Lying there with Vanessa asleep on my chest, her breaths soft and rhythmic, I found myself lost in thought, my mind drifting through the maze of memories and emotions she stirred within me.

I remembered the first time I saw her. It was at Griff's gym. She was putting up a fuss at the front desk. She had this energy about her, a vibrancy that you couldn't ignore. I remember thinking she was trouble - the best kind of trouble. The kind I liked to get into.

Since then, every moment with her had been like a shot of adrenaline, a mix of excitement and unpredictability. But tonight, as I held her in my arms, I realized shit was deeper than I cared to admit. But damn, everything about her was right. The way she laughed, the way she looked at me, the way she challenged me - it all resonated in a place deep within me that I rarely let anyone touch.

I closed my eyes, letting the memories of my time with her wash over me. There were so many moments, snapshots in time, where I caught glimpses of something more between us. The way she'd look at me when she thought I wasn't watching, the softness in her voice when she'd talk about something she was passionate about, the fire in her eyes when she argued with me. All these things painted a picture of a woman who was complex, strong, and so damn captivating.

But there was a complication, a significant one - Vince Mutherfuckin' Cartwright. I knew dude. I mean, I didn't know him like that, but I knew him. I met him through Griff. He helped save Vanessa and Gabby when they were kidnapped last year, and he'd stuck around. We were cool. I respected dude; he seemed like a good man. Problem was he had feelings for my girl. And the bigger problem was that my girl felt some type of way about him too. And the crazy thing was that me and ol' boy knew what was up. There was just an unspoken thing between us, a silent acknowledgment of our mutual affection to her. But tonight, watching him dance with my girl, something shifted within me. For me, this thing with Vanessa was no longer a simple attraction; it was a deep, gnawing need to be hers and have her be mine.

Wait.

Did I just... my girl?

I sighed, running a hand through my hair. This was uncharted territory for me. I was used to casual, uncomplicated. Vanessa was anything but uncomplicated. She had layers upon layers, and I found myself wanting to explore each one, no matter how deep I had to go.

As I lay there, with her warmth seeping into me, a mixture of contentment and turmoil settled in my chest. This woman, sleeping so peacefully against me, had somehow become my calm and my storm. How had I, Gage Emerson, the man who avoided complications with females like the plague, found myself here? Wanting, needing someone as free as the wind and as fierce as a hurricane?

The moonlight filtered through the window, casting a soft glow on Vanessa's face. She looked so serene, so beautiful, it made my chest tighten. And in that moment, I knew. No matter how this played out, no matter what complications lay ahead, I was too deep to back out now.

CHAPTER FOUR

VANESSA

The aroma of freshly brewed coffee and the soft murmur of conversations surrounded me as I walked into Sips-N-Kicks, me and Gabby's go-to spot for anything from venting sessions to serious life discussions. The cozy coffee shop, nestled in the heart of the Park District, was like a second home, a place where I could always find comfort—and today, I needed it more than ever.

I spotted Gabby at our usual table, her smile bright as she waved me over. Despite the upbeat atmosphere of the shop, I felt a knot of anxiety in my stomach. I had only just parted from Gage an hour ago, and he was still heavy on my mind. I really was surprised to pull up last night and find him parked in my driveway. And the way he sexed me down put a bitch right to sleep. And this morning! He woke me up with that talented mouth of his slowly, almost lazily lapping at my pussy. A shiver passed through me at the thought.

"Morning, bestie," I greeted Gabby, sliding into the chair across from her.

"Hey, V. I ordered you an apple crisp macchiato," she said, sliding a drink across the table.

My mouth split into the biggest smile. Damn, I loved my bestie. I grabbed the cup. "Thanks, booskie," I said before taking a sip.

"You're welcome. It's the least I could do after that amazing party you threw us last night. We had so much fun." She reached out and covered my hand, which was resting on the table. "Thank you, V. Seriously... thank you."

Her words had me feeling all warm inside. "Of course. You know I got you. And we both know I don't do nothin' half-assed." I added with a chuckle.

Gabby rolled her eyes dramatically. "You're a mess."

"And you love me for it," I told her.

She laughed. "And do."

We were quiet for a minute as we sipped our coffee, and my thoughts immediately went to the sexy ass grin on Gage's face as he winked and waved goodbye as he got into his car this morning. I swear that man was a sexual gladiator. The way he stretched me out with that glorious dick of his last night and then this morning, waking up to his mouth on my pussy and then fucking in the shower, it's a wonder I could even walk.

"Hey," Gabby called, tapping her finger on the table.

"Huh? What?" I responded, focusing my gaze on her.

Her brows furrowed as she studied me. "What's going on, V?"

I gave her an incredulous look as I shrugged and shook my head at her. "What do you mean? We're about to discuss your wedding."

Gabby cocked her head to the side and pursed her lips at me. "And we'll get to that after you tell me what's going on. You seem a little distracted. Is this about last night?" She asked.

I nearly choked on the sip of coffee I'd taken. "W-what? Last night?" I spurted. How the hell did she know Gage was at my house? Did he tell her or Griff he was stopping by? I mean, if he did, that's cool. It's Gabby. I would have probably told her anyway.

My mind was racing, and it was all ridiculous.

"Hello? Vanessa," Gabby called as she snapped her fingers in the space between us. "Girl, please. What is going on with you?"

"I'm sorry. I... I think I'm just a little tired is all. You know Gage was in my driveway when I got home last night," I replied.

Gabby's brows lifted. "Really?"

I scrunched my face at her. "Yeah. You didn't know? You mentioned last night, so I thought-"

She cut me off. "I was talking about you having to juggle Gage and Vince at the party. You were a little anxious last night. I was worried about you."

"Oh, that. Yeah, that was... I don't know what that was. I was trippin'," I told her, downplaying my distress.

Gabby wasn't having it. She knew me too well to believe my bullshit. "Tell that to someone who hasn't been your bestie for umpteen years."

I rolled my eyes and took a sip of my coffee.

"You can roll them eyes if you want to, but we're not doing anything until you talk to me about what's going on with you and your men."

I sighed. "Fine." As I settled into the conversation, I felt the weight of my recent encounters pressing on me. The memory of Gage's touch lingered on my skin. The memory of Vince's hands on my lower back as we danced. Both were sending conflicting signals to my heart and mind.

"I don't know, Gabbs. I'm still trying to wrap my head around it. You know me. I've always dated around and had fun, nothing serious. But now... with those two, things are different," I told her.

Gabby looked at me like she wanted to say something but was holding back.

"What?" I urged her.

She shrugged. "I don't know, V. It's just... look, I know you. I know how you roll when it comes to men and relationships. You don't do them. You never have. You like your freedom, but..."

I leaned my elbows on the table. I wanted to hear what she had to say. "What? Just say it."

"Everyone can see that you have deep feelings for both Gage and Vince. I think we were all just waiting for you to realize it and then make a choice," she said.

I was shocked. First of all, why were folks watching my moves close enough to make assumptions about my love life? Second... hell, who was I kidding? There was no second. Whoever the folks, all in my business were, were right. I did have deep feelings for both men. I just had no idea what to do about it. Shit was confusing.

I blew out a breath, then rolled my lips between my teeth. My feelings were so messy I really didn't know what to say.

"V," Gabby started, her expression one of understanding and concern. "Talk to me. I know you, and I know this has to be driving you crazy."

She was right about that. Shit was definitely making me bonkers. I'd spent too much time obsessing over it lately. Maybe I needed a second opinion.

I took a long swig of my coffee, then said, "I don't know, Gabby, it's like... I have all these feelings... deep feelings and emotions about both of them. And it's crazy because it's not like I feel more for one than the other. My feelings run the same for both men and I'm just confused because how is that possible?"

Gabby's gaze softened further as she looked at me. "Anything is possible when it comes to love, V."

I reared back. "Love? Who said anything about love? I'm just experiencing feelings I've never felt before. That's all," I argued.

"Umm-hmm," was all Gabby said.

I sighed. "Seriously. Gabby, I'm not even sure I know what love is."

It was Gabby's turn to look at me crazy. "Bitch, what? You know good and well what love is. You're surrounded by it every day. You exude it. V, you been loving me since we were kids-"

I cut her off. "That's not the same, and you know it."

"Okay, fine. I'll give you that, but it's still love. You know what love is, V? Love is wanting what's best for someone. It's deeply feeling their joy when they're happy and feeling it even harder when they're sad. It's missing them when they're not with you. It's smiling at the memory of a touch or a conversation. It's feeling restful in your own spirit when you know your person is okay. It's instinctual. It's felt here," she pointed to my chest. "Not here," she finished, pointing to my head.

Damn. When she put it like that, I guess I did know what love was. But to feel it with two different men?

"Okay, say I do know what love is. Can you be in love with two people at once? Like *really* be in love with both of them?" I asked.

"Stranger things have happened. Look at me. I didn't plan on falling in love last year, and we both know some crazy shit happened to even put that in motion," she said.

She was referring to how she met and fell in love with Griff. They met because she was being harassed to sell her flower shop and was too stubborn to go to the police for help, so I suggested she take self-defense classes at Griff's gym. They met under really crazy circumstances, and things only got crazier as they got to know each other. I'm talkin' about a break-in at Gabby's shop, us being kidnapped, Griff, his security team, and Vince rescuing us, and then finding out Griff's uncle was behind the whole thing. It was a mess, but through it all, Gabby and Griff's bond only got stronger. And look at them now, engaged and about to be married.

"I get what you're saying, but my situation is different. It's two, let me say that again, two guys, and...I-I've fallen for them both for very different reasons. It's so confusing, Gab."

"I can imagine. Have you talked to each guy about the other?"

I immediately frowned, and Gabby put her hand up to stop me from popping off.

"I'm only asking because of what I saw at the party last night, your interactions with Gage at dinner, and that dance with Vince. Phew!" Gabby fanned herself. "They were both there. I know they saw what I saw. Plus, they had eyes on you all night. How could they not?"

I took a deep breath, considering what she said. I didn't realize the attraction between me and the guys was so palpable. But I knew she was right. If others at the party noticed it, I'm sure Gage and Vince did too. Funny, neither guy said a word about it. Not Vince when I talked to him at my car in the parking lot or Gage last night at my house or this morning.

"I mean, when you put it like that, I'm sure they have an idea. But they know me. They know how I am when it comes to relationships. I don't officially do them, and I've never made it a habit of talking to the men I date about the other men I date. So..."

"I get that, but this is different, V. You really like them. Like *really* like them. I can tell. And it's causing you stress. You need to figure it out."

"I know," I agreed in defeat. "I'm... I'm just not ready to have that conversation yet." I confessed.

"I know, friend, but listen," Gabby said, her voice firm yet gentle. "You're one of the strongest people I know. You'll work this out in your own way, in your own time. And guess what?"

"What?"

"Imma be right there with you, holding you up. Whatever you do, I got you," she said.

Her words were like a balm to my chaotic thoughts. I nodded, feeling a bit more grounded. "Thanks, boo. See, this is why you my bestie."

"And always will be," Gabby threw in.

"Fa' sho! Now, enough of my soap opera. Let's get to these wedding plans," I said.

As we turned our attention to the wedding, discussing themes and decorations, I couldn't help but feel grateful for Gabby. She was more than a friend; she was my anchor in the storm that was my love life. And right now, I needed that anchor more than ever.

Gabby and I got a lot done when we finally focused on why we were there - her wedding. We finalized the wedding colors and the invitations and narrowed the caterer down to two. By the time we packed up to leave, we were feeling really good about our progress. Gabby hadn't wanted to use a wedding planner, so we were doing it together, and I thought we were doing a damn good job. And the best thing is that I was so preoccupied with wedding plans that I didn't think of my crazy love life. However, that couldn't be said for my drive to the office.

I pulled my car into my reserved spot in front of my office and got out. The moment I stepped into Davis & Associates, the law firm I started with one of my close friends from law school, my switch flipped. Vanessa Davis, the woman wrestling with a tangled love life, receded into the background. In her place stood Vanessa Davis, Esq., sharp-minded and ready to conquer the legal world.

My heels clicked authoritatively against the polished marble floor as I made my way to my office. My assistant, Marissa, greeted me with a stack of messages and a brief rundown of my schedule. "Your 10 AM with the Johnsons is waiting in the conference room," she informed me.

"Thanks, Marissa. Any updates on the Henderson case?" I asked, swiftly shifting gears to my cases.

"We got the deposition transcripts. There are a few inconsistencies we can use," she replied. Her efficiency was one of the many reasons I value her so much.

I nodded, pleased. "Good work. Let's push for a settlement meeting. I think they might be ready to fold."

Settling into the rhythm of work, I navigated through meetings, phone calls, and strategy sessions with a focused precision. My colleagues respected my tenacity, and my clients appreciated my empathetic yet no-nonsense approach. Each legal puzzle I solved, each victory I clinched for a client, added to the sense of fulfillment my career brought me.

But even amidst the legal jargon and the strategic planning, my mind would occasionally drift to Gage's electrifying touch or Vince's intense gaze. Their presence in my life was like an undercurrent, subtle yet persistent, pulling at me even in my most focused moments.

During a brief respite in my office, I gazed out at the bustling cityscape. The view from the 20th floor was always a reminder of how far I'd come - from a little girl in Eastbrook dreaming of making a difference to a woman who was actually doing it. Yet, here I was, a successful attorney, still trying to decipher the complexities of my heart.

A tap at my door pulled me from my thoughts. It was Marissa, accompanying a young woman who looked familiar. "Ms. Davis, this is Kara, Mr. Franklin's niece. She has some documents for you."

"Ah, yes, Kara, please come in. How's your uncle?" I asked, recalling the pro bono work I did for her family's business.

"He's better, thanks to you. We couldn't have

navigated the legal mess without your help," she said, her gratitude evident.

I smiled warmly at her. "It was nothing, really. You know how I feel about this community. I'm always happy to help the people of Eastbrook."

She nodded. "I know. That's why so many of us look up to you. Gabby too. Thanks again, Vanessa. I'll see you around."

As Kara left, her words lingered. I helped her family find a solution that worked for everyone involved, a win-win situation. If only my personal life were that straightforward.

The rest of the day passed in a blur of legalities and client meetings. As the city lights began to twinkle alive outside my window, I sat back in my chair, my mind returning to Gage and Vince.

Navigating my feelings for them felt like wading through uncharted waters. Could there be a win-win solution in my love life too? Or was I destined to make a choice that would leave part of my heart wanting?

My heart? What was I even saying? In all my years of dating, my heart never factored into the equation. So, why now?

Sighing, I gathered my things. Maybe the answers lay somewhere outside the confines of my office, somewhere in the unpredictable rhythm of life.

CHAPTER FIVE

VINCE

The crisp sound of my dress shoes echoed off the sleek, modern walls of S & T Security Firm's Eastbrook office. Stepping inside, the contrast between my past life as a detective with Eastbrook PD and my new reality couldn't be starker. High-tech gadgets buzzed softly in the background, and an air of controlled urgency pervaded the space. This place, with its blend of cutting-edge technology and palpable tension, was a world away from the clear-cut boundaries of police work.

I made my way to my office, a space that was more utilitarian than the lavish decor of the reception area. Here, the walls were adorned with maps and monitors displaying various security feeds. My desk was a testament to organized chaos, with files and notes about ongoing cases.

Sitting down, I leaned back in my chair, allowing myself a moment to take it all in. The offer from Sigma and Trace had come at a time when I was questioning my future with the force. The pay was more than double what I earned as a detective, but it wasn't just about the money – it was the freedom. Here, I wasn't bound by red tape and bureaucratic hurdles. I could actually make a difference without my hands being tied. But with that freedom came a price – operating in the grey areas, something I was still wrestling with. Every decision now came with its own set of ethical dilemmas, making me question the lines I was willing to cross.

I glanced at a photo on my desk, a group shot from my days at the precinct. Those days were simpler in some ways. Although not all law enforcement followed the rules, my moral compass was firmly set. Now, the lines were blurred, and every decision came with its own set of ethical questions.

Sigma and Trace had made it clear when they recruited me – their operations weren't always by the book, but they were effective. They'd seen something in me, something even I hadn't fully recognized – a knack for seeing beyond the black and white, for understanding that sometimes justice needed a different approach. I learned that last year when Vanessa and Gabby were abducted. I worked with Sigma, Trace, and Griff to find them, and let's just say the twins had their own unique methods of getting things done.

A soft knock on the door pulled me from my thoughts. I straightened up, slipping into my professional persona. "Come in," I called out.

Yara, my assistant, stepped in, her efficiency a stark contrast to the chaos of the streets I used to patrol.

"Morning, Vince. You've got a meeting with Sigma in ten, and Trace wants to brief you on the new surveillance setup for the Prizler case afterward," Yara informed me, her tone brisk yet friendly.

I nodded, appreciative of her knack for keeping my schedule running smoothly. "Thanks, Yara. Any updates from the field team on the West End project?"

"They checked in an hour ago. All clear, no suspicious activities. They'll continue monitoring throughout the day," she replied, scanning her notes.

"Good. Keep me posted," I said, my mind already shifting gears to the day's agenda. The West End project was delicate – a fine line between ensuring community safety and respecting boundaries. It was a balance I was still learning to strike in this new role.

Yara left, closing the door softly behind her. I took a moment, my thoughts drifting to Vanessa. She had been on my mind since last night, since that dance that had felt more like a moment suspended in time. From day one, there was an undeniable connection between us, something that went beyond physical attraction. It felt as if she was a part of me, of my soul. Everything in me wanted to see her happy, satisfied, and protected. And while we never had the whole "feelings" conversation, I knew she was feeling me just as much. Only problem is, she was feeling someone else too - Gage Emerson.

Gage was a good dude. Loud, funny, charming, and as a championship boxer, he commanded every room he was in. I knew he was seeing Vanessa too, and there was nothing I could do about that. I didn't even want to, really. Vanessa and I weren't in a committed relationship, and no matter how badly I wanted her in that way, I wouldn't press her on it. She loved her freedom and doing things her own way, in her own time, and I respected that. That didn't mean that knowing she spent time with another man didn't bother me a bit. As a detective, I was trained to observe, to notice the subtle cues and unspoken words, and it was clear to see Vanessa and Gage's connection at the engagement party. They had a real playful, flirty, but deep connection, and I wondered what that meant for her and me.

Shaking off the thought, I stood up, adjusting my jacket. My meeting with Sigma was starting in two minutes. As I walked to the meeting room, I mentally prepared myself. Working with Sigma and Trace was a constant learning curve, a challenge I had come to relish.

In this new world, I had found a place where my skills as a detective were valued, but more importantly, where I could operate with a freedom I had never known. It was a world of grey, and I was slowly finding my shade.

I stepped into the conference room, finding Sigma and Trace already there, their attention focused on multiple screens displaying various security feeds. The air was charged with a silent intensity unique to them. Sigma, leaning back in his chair with an easy grace, and Trace, his eyes scanning the screens with a meticulous gaze, both embodied the duality of our firm's approach – charm and strategy, force and precision.

"Vince, what up, man?" Sigma greeted, his voice carrying that familiar, confident timbre.

"Morning," I greeted back with a head nod to him, then Trace.

Trace gave a slight nod, his greeting more reserved but equally welcoming. "We've got a new assignment. It's right up your alley," he said, gesturing towards the screen displaying a complex layout of what looked like an industrial compound.

I leaned forward, examining the details. "What's the play?" I asked, my detective instincts kicking in.

Sigma stood up, walking over to the screen. "High-risk extraction. A client's daughter got caught up in a bad situation. We need to get her out without causing an international incident."

I listened, my mind already running through possible scenarios and strategies. This was the kind of challenge I thrived on – complex, demanding a blend of intellect and action. It was this blend that Sigma and Trace had recognized in me a year ago.

I remembered the day they approached me.

I was at a crossroads in my career, feeling increasingly constrained by the limitations of police work. Sigma and Trace laid out their vision, speaking of a world where results mattered more than procedures, where my skills could be fully utilized without bureaucratic handcuffs.

"We've seen you in action, Vince. You've got a sharp mind and make really thoughtful decisions in a pinch, even if that decision teeters the line," Sigma had said, his words resonating with an undeniable truth.

Trace, who really only spoke when he had something profound to say, had added, "We operate in grey areas, Vince. It's not for everyone. But we think you're cut out for it. Think about it – no more red tape, no more playing by rules that don't get results."

I was brought back to the present by Sigma's voice. "What do you think? You wanna head this one up with me?"

I nodded, a sense of resolve settling in. "Yeah. When do we start?"

"Tomorrow," Sigma said, then turned to Trace. "Pull up the details, Trace.

Trace leaned forward, tapping on the screen, bringing up images and files. "Here's what we know," Sigma started. "The target, Dijana, is the daughter of a high-profile Serbian diplomat. She's being held in this compound," he pointed at a satellite image of a heavily guarded facility.

"Our intel suggests the facility is owned by a faction of the Serbian cartel, but we haven't confirmed that yet. Her father has made quite a few enemies with his backing of the crackdown on organized crime in the country, and he thinks that she was taken because of that."

"Where was she taken from? Was she here in the States or Serbia?" I asked.

"Serbia. They snatched her while hanging out with friends and brought her over here. My bet is that they plan to sell her into the sex trade. And you know if they do that, the chances of getting her back are slim to none."

I nodded. He was right. Kidnap victims were almost impossible to find after about 72 hours. We needed to move on this.

I studied the layout, noting entry and exit points and potential blind spots. "Surveillance first. We need eyes on the inside. Figure out their routines, shifts, any weaknesses."

Sigma nodded in agreement. "We're setting up deep surveillance tonight. You'll oversee that with Trace while I get the gear, supplies, and transportation situated. We need a full report by noon tomorrow. I want to head out by three. We'll take the jet, which should get us to Kentucky in about an hour and a half."

The next hour was a flurry of planning. The compound was located in a remote, heavily wooded area. We dissected every detail of the exterior of the compound and surrounding areas, from escape routes to contingency plans.

After the meeting, I stayed back with Trace to review the Prizler case's new surveillance setup.

This was a different beast – a local case involving corporate espionage. "The new cams are up. We'll get alerts on any unusual activities," Trace explained.

"Good. Let's keep this clean. Jerry Prizler is relying on us to get his company's data back without any legal blowback," I responded, my mind already strategizing the next steps.

"Always. I got a few tweaks to make, but we're good," Trace said, his fingers flying over the keyboard.

"Bet. I'mma head to my office to finish up a few things. What time you wanna link up for surveillance? I asked.

"Eleven," Trace replied, his eyes glued to the monitor.

Leaving Trace to do his thing, I headed back to my office. Of course, my thoughts wandered back to Vanessa. Picking up my phone, I hesitated for a moment before typing out a message:

Me: Early dinner tonight? I know a place that has the best seafood in town.

Vanessa: Sir! I know every seafood place in town, and they're all average at best.   lol!

Me: Girl, stop being extra and have dinner with me. I'mma be out of pocket for a few days and want to see you before I go.

Vanessa: Well, in that case, I'm there. What time?

Me: I'll scoop you at 4:30.

Vanessa: Oh, you mean an early-early dinner. I'll still be at the office. Come swoop me here.

Me: Bet. See you later.

Setting my phone down, I stared out the window, the cityscape sprawling before me. In this new world of grey, I had found a place where my skills were valued, but more importantly, where I could operate with a freedom I had never known. Yet, as I gazed out, my thoughts were on Vanessa – fierce, independent, smart as shit, funny, caring, and caught between me and Gage. Visions of them at the party - the chemistry, the connection was real and it had me wondering about our future. Could there be a real place for me in her life, or was I setting myself up for something that could never be?

CHAPTER SIX

GAGE

The rhythmic thud of my gloves against the heavy bag echoed through Griff's gym, a familiar soundtrack to the grueling sessions that had become my second home. As each punch landed, the sound mingled with the distant clatter of weights and the low hum of other fighters' determination, grounding me in the moment yet reminding me of the stakes—personal and professional.

Griff, standing a few feet away, watched every move with the eyes of a hawk. "Come on, Gage, dig deeper! That bag's not going to hit back, but your opponent will," he called out. His words, laden with years of experience and a shared history, pushed me beyond physical exhaustion, touching a nerve that was already frayed by thoughts of Vanessa.

I grunted in response, my fists finding a new rhythm, harder and faster. There was a reason Griff was fast becoming known as one of the best trainers around. He pushed you beyond limits. As a retired professional boxer, he knew what it took to be a champion, and he poured all of that into how he trained fighters. He didn't just train boxers; he forged champions. And more than that, he was a friend. Like a real fucking friend. He believed in me and never shied away from calling me on my shit. I appreciated that about him.

As I launched into a series of rapid jabs, my mind flickered to the upcoming fight. This wasn't just another match; it was the pinnacle of everything I'd worked for. A victory here could solidify my career and catapult me to new heights.

"Focus, Gage! Technique is just as important as power," Griff shouted, stepping closer to hold the bag steady.

I nodded, adjusting my stance. Griff was right. In this game, brawn needed to be balanced with brains. As I threw a combination of punches, I could feel the burn in my muscles, the sweet pain of progress. But as much as I tried to focus solely on the fight, my thoughts kept drifting to Vanessa. Her laugh, her sass, the way she looked at me sometimes... it was enough to throw any man off his game. She had slipped under my skin, into my head, and now, into my fucking heart.

It wasn't like me to get distracted, especially not in the middle of training. But Vanessa wasn't just any distraction. She was a whirlwind, a force of nature that had taken me by surprise.

"Alright, take five," Griff called out, signaling the end of the round.

I peeled off my gloves, grabbing a towel to wipe

the sweat from my face. As I took a swig of water, I could feel Griff's eyes on me, his expression a mix of curiosity and concern.

"What's up, man? You training hard, your forms A-1, but something's off. What's goin' on?" he asked, leaning against the ring.

I hesitated, then decided to be honest. "It's Vanessa," I admitted, feeling a mix of frustration and longing at just mentioning her name.

Griff nodded, not surprised. "Ah. Feisty-ass Vanessa. She got yo ass in a chokehold."

I smirked and waved him off. "Man, fuck you."

Griff shook his head at me. "Am I wrong, my nigga?" He asked.

I shrugged, the complexity of my feelings for Vanessa hard to put into words. "Shit. I don't know. This girl got my shit all kinds of fucked up."

Griff chuckled softly. "Love will do that to you, man. That love shit, it's a hell of a fighter. Hits harder than any opponent you'll face in the ring."

I laughed despite the turmoil inside. "That's a hell of an analogy."

Griff nodded. "It's true though. This love shit will have you turned inside out. Trust, I know."

And he did. Gabby had my boy all kinds of caught up last year. I watched the shit happen. I knew what it looked like, even if I didn't want to admit it.

"Use it," Griff suggested, a serious note in his voice. "Let whatever you're feeling for her drive you. Channel it into your training, into the fight.

It's what I did when Gabby went missing. I pushed all those feelings into finding her."

I nodded, a new sense of determination settling in. Griff was right. I couldn't let my feelings for Vanessa weaken me. Instead, I had to let them fuel me and push me.

As I slipped my gloves back on, I felt a renewed focus. Whatever was going on with Vanessa, I would face it head-on, just like I did with every challenge in my life. But right now, I had a fight to prepare for, and nothing was going to stop me from winning.

Griff and I went round after round in the ring, my fight fueled by all the fucked up and chaotic emotions swirling in my head. By the time Griff called an end to our session, we were both panting and drenched in sweat.

"I see you took my advice and used that shit," Griff commented as he tossed me a towel.

I just smirked as I wiped sweat from my face.

Just then, the door swung open, and Vanessa walked in. Her arrival was like a jolt of electricity, her presence instantly transforming the space. As she walked in, the air shifted, charged with an energy that both excited and unnerved me. It was as if her confidence and laughter breathed life into the sterile gym atmosphere, making the air lighter and my gloves heavier all at once.

"What's goin' on, fellas," she greeted, her eyes finding mine. At that moment, the world narrowed to just the two of us, her gaze igniting a spark that threatened to consume me whole.

"What's up, V? What brings you down here? Ready to start training with me?" Griff asked with a chuckle.

Vanessa flashed a haughty smirk at him. "Don't play with me, Griffin Thayer. I'll have your ass chasing me all over that ring. Keep talking shit."

"You got it, V," Griff said with a grin as he lifted his hands in surrender and backed away. "I'mma hit the shower. I'll check you later, Gage. Vanessa, good to see you as always."

Griff excused himself, leaving me and Vanessa alone. She stared up at me with those gorgeous-ass expressive eyes, and my fucking heart stuttered. Fuck! This woman had the power to knock me off balance with just a look.

I hopped out of the ring, my eyes roaming over her curvy body. She looked so fucking good in the dark denim jeans that hugged her round ass and the cropped sweater that showed off a sliver of her flat stomach. Had my shit on instant rock.

"Looks like you put in some real work today," she said, eyeing my sweat-drenched body.

"Tried to," I managed, still catching my breath. "It helps to have something... or someone... to push you. Even when they're not here."

Her eyes softened, a hint of something more behind her casual demeanor. "I get that. Pushing yourself for something... or someone... that matters makes all the difference."

The way she said it, the slight emphasis on

'someone,' sent a ripple of excitement through me. It was like an unspoken acknowledgment of the uncharted territory we were navigating together.

I stepped closer, closing the space between us. "Vanessa..." I began, feeling a jumble of emotions I couldn't quite name.

She raised a hand, her touch light on my chest. "Gage, I know. I know. But... let's not worry about... about those things right now. You have a big fight coming up, and that should be your focus. But I'm here. I'm with you."

Her words, simple yet profound, eased the knot of tension in my gut. She was right. I needed to focus on my upcoming fight. And I would. I knew what she meant, and I knew she was here for me. I wanted her with me in Vegas too.

"Come to Vegas with me for the fight," I said, deliberately not making it a question.

She bit into that luscious bottom lip as she grinned up at me. "Was that a question or..."

I ran my knuckles along her jawline down to her chin, then lightly pinched it between my fingers. "Yo lil ass always playing. You coming with me to Vegas for the fight or nah?" This time it was a question.

"You know I wouldn't miss it. Besides, someone has to make sure you're not just lounging around poolside in Vegas," she teased, her eyes twinkling with humor.

I laughed, feeling a warmth spread through me at the thought of her being there. "Oh trust, there'll be some lounging poolside, just after I handle my business."

She raised an eyebrow, a playful challenge in her gaze. "Yeah, you better handle business. I don't fuck with losers."

I draped an arm around her waist and tugged her against me as I slid my hand from her chin to her throat and wrapped my fingers around it. I moved my thumb under her chin and lifted, locking her gaze on mine. "Well, that's a good thing cuz you and I both know I ain't no fuckin' loser, sweetheart."

"Oh, I know. I just gotta keep you on your toes, Daddy," she smirked.

My dick jumped at her calling me Daddy. "You better be glad we in a gym full of people because I'd have your ass bent over the side of this ring with my dick buried so deep in that tight ass pussy, you'd feel my shit in your throat."

"Shit, Gage. What the hell you tryna do to me?" Vanessa asked, trying to lean back, but I had her captive.

I ground my hips into her. "What it feel like?"

"Oh, my God. You're so bad, and I gotta go. I have a meeting to get to. It's not too far from here, which is why I stopped by."

I wasn't ready to let her go just yet. As she leaned in for a quick peck, I caught her bottom lip between my teeth and sucked. She moaned, and I thrust my tongue deep into her mouth before capturing her tongue and sucking on it. She tasted so fucking good. So damn sweet. I licked, sucked, and nipped at her mouth until she was breathless and rubbing her pussy against my shit.

I pulled back from the kiss and stared down into her pretty face. Her brown eyes had turned to a warm golden color and shone with a need that had me wanting to drag her into the locker room and fuck her in one of the private shower stalls. But, she had to go. She had a meeting to get to, and I knew how much her work meant to her. So, I kept my eyes open and locked on hers as I pressed a gentle kiss to her lips. That simple kiss spoke volumes more than words ever could, and I knew she knew it because her breathing picked up, and I could feel the chill run through her body. For a moment, we stood there, suspended in time, just looking at each other, a silent conversation passing between us. One of understanding, of something deep between us that neither of us had anticipated but couldn't move around from.

"I umm... I should go. I have that meeting," she stammered.

"Yep. I'll hit you up," I told her, then placed a kiss on her forehead.

"Bye, Gage," she said, then headed for the exit.

Watching her leave, the gym suddenly felt too quiet, too empty, even though there were people working out throughout the space. Griff's earlier words echoed in my head, "Love will do that to you, man." It was a truth I was only beginning to understand, a fight I was unprepared for but somehow eager to face.

Her words, 'I'm here, I'm with you,' reverberated in my mind. It was spoken with such sincerity and felt like a lifeline and a challenge all at once. It was a promise that filled the spaces between my jumbled thoughts and racing heart, grounding me yet urging me to reach for something beyond victory in the ring.

Alone, surrounded by the remnants of our encounter, I was left to ponder the future. The connection with Vanessa, so unexpected and intense, had become a force I couldn't ignore. It wasn't just about winning the fight anymore; it was about navigating this new emotional landscape she had unveiled.

As I headed to the locker room to shower, I realized that whatever was happening between Vanessa and me was something special. Something that I couldn't, and didn't want to, ignore.

CHAPTER SEVEN

VANESSA

I curled up on my couch, the soft cream fabric a stark contrast to the jumbled mess of thoughts in my head. A half-filled journal lay open on my lap, the pen in my hand idle as I struggled to make sense of the chaos in my heart. I'd always been the one with words, but now, they eluded me, like shadows flitting just out of reach.

With a deep breath, I forced the pen onto the paper, trying to spill out the mess in my mind.

"Gage and Vince... Two sides of a coin I keep flipping, unable to decide where it lands. With Gage, it's laughter and excitement, a rush of adrenaline every time I see him. His smile, the way he looks at me – it's like being caught in a warm, vibrant dance."

I paused, the pen hovering over the paper as I thought about Vince. The quiet strength he carried, the way his eyes seemed to see right into the deepest parts of me. There's a sense of safety with him, a calmness that complements the storm in my soul.

"But Vince... he's the quiet after the storm, the deep waters that promise both peace and depth. When he holds me, there's a sense of coming home, a safety that

I didn't know I was seeking."

I let out a shaky breath, the weight of my emotions bearing down on me. How could I feel so much for both of them? It was like walking a tightrope between two skyscrapers, each step fraught with the fear of falling, yet unable to resist the exhilarating journey.

"I'm so torn. With Gage, I fly; with Vince, I dive deep. How can I choose between soaring and diving? How can I tell one that my heart aches for the other just as fiercely?

The pen fell from my fingers, and I leaned back, my eyes brimming with unshed tears. Fuck! I'm in love. Deeply, with two men who couldn't be more different, yet both were essential to me in ways I could barely articulate.

Closing the journal, I sat in silence, the echo of my unvoiced fears filling the room. I knew I couldn't keep walking this line forever. But for now, I clung to this fragile in-between, where love was as confusing as it was beautiful, as overwhelming as it was liberating.

I glanced at the clock on my cell. I had thirty minutes before I had to meet Gage at the Urban Chef for a cooking class. I quickly finished my makeup, fluffed out my natural, and headed out the door.

Gage was already in the parking lot when I pulled up. My mouth watered at the sight of him. He looked so damn good. He was dressed casually in a pair of fatigue-colored cargo pants, a white tee with a red and white plaid flannel, and some red and white Jordans. He was leaning against his truck, looking at his cell.

"What's up, handsome," I greeted as I walked up.

"Dimples," he said with a grin as his eyes took me in from head to toe. He pocketed his phone and reached for me, pulling me in for a hug. "You look beautiful, as always," he complimented. "You ready to cook some shit?"

I chuckled as I stared up at him. "Yep! Let's do it."

He stared down at me for a second, then kissed me gently on the lips. "Let's go," he said, then grabbed my hand and led me into the building.

The warm glow of the cooking studio welcomed us, its cozy ambiance a sharp contrast to the crisp evening outside. Gage and I stepped in, greeted by the rich aroma of herbs and baking dough. The class tonight was about crafting gourmet pizzas from scratch, a choice I'd made hoping for some light-hearted fun with Gage. His infectious energy always turned the most mundane activities into adventures.

"We making pizza? Oh, I got this," Gage boasted.

"Okay, Chef-Boy-R-G. Let's not get ahead of ourselves," I clowned.

Gage frowned at me. "Girl, I love pizza. Eat it all the time; therefore, I think I'll make the best pizza."

I rolled my eyes playfully. "I guess we'll just have to wait and see."

We joined a small group gathered around a large table laden with ingredients. Flour, yeast, an array of toppings – everything we needed was right there, inviting us to dive into the culinary challenge.

The instructor, a jovial man with a thick Italian accent, began the class, guiding us through the steps of kneading and rolling our dough. Gage, with his boxer's strength, took to the kneading with a gusto that had me in stitches. Flour dusted his cheeks, and he looked adorably clueless yet determined.

"Watch and learn, Vanessa," he teased, flexing his arms theatrically as he worked the dough. "These are the hands of a champion – in the ring and the kitchen."

I rolled my eyes playfully, joining him in the kneading process. Our elbows bumped, and every accidental touch sent a spark through me. We chose our toppings, and Gage playfully loaded my pizza with an extra heap of cheese, earning a mock glare from me.

"Hey, I'm just making sure you get the best pizza experience," he said, his laughter echoing around the room.

As our pizzas baked, we joined the other participants at a large table, sharing stories and sips of wine. Gage's laugh was infectious, his charm effortless. He had this way of making everyone feel like they were old friends.

But amidst the laughter, my mind wandered. Here I was, having an amazing time with Gage, yet part of me ached with guilt. Vince's face flashed in my mind, his steady gaze, the way he held me like I was something precious. The contrast between them was stark – Gage with his vibrant energy, Vince with his calming presence. How could my heart yearn for both so equally?

As we took the first bites of our handmade pizzas, Gage's creation was surprisingly good, and I couldn't help but admire him. He caught me staring and winked. "Told you, my pizza would be fire."

And it was. The tangy sweetness of the tomato sauce, the creamy richness of melted mozzarella, the herbs he used, and the slight char of the perfectly baked crust were explosive. His pizza was lowkey better than mine.

"Yeah, you did," I concurred.

"Ya man's is full of surprises, girl," Gage joked.

"Yeah, you are," I murmured, my voice softer than I intended.

Gage set his pizza down as he studied me. He wiped his hands and then pulled me against him. He tucked a finger under my chin and lifted, connecting my gaze with his.

"You got a little sauce..." he said, as he dipped his head and licked the corner of my mouth. Tingles flooded my body, and juices flooded my panties. "Mmm. This sauce tastes so much better on you."

I grinned. "Oh yeah?"

He nodded.

"Well, I bet it tastes just as good on you. Should we find out?" I teased.

Gage's nostrils flared, and he quickly released me. I watched as he boxed up our remaining pizza, grabbed the bowl of sauce, and then my hand.

I laughed. "What are you doing?"

"We bout to put your theory to the test." He looked at our instructor. "We bout to head out. Thanks, man. This was a great class." He looked back at me. "Let's go, dimples."

We left my car in the parking lot and took Gage's truck to his place. He'd purchased a unit in the same luxury high-rise that Griff lived in. We were barely through the door before we were pulling at each other's clothes.

I slipped Gage's flannel off, then his white tee. I bit down into my lip at the sight of his smooth skin pulled taunt over hard muscle. My eyes roamed over his tatts, my tongue itching to taste them. I made a move to do just that, but Gage stopped me, circling my throat with one of his big hands. He brought his face close to mine, his warm breath fanning across my lips.

"You was talking shit earlier about how good this sauce would taste on me." He flicked out his tongue and ran it across my lips, and I whimpered. "You wanna test that theory?" He trailed his lips from my mouth along my jawline and up to my ear. "I think you do. Get on your knees, gorgeous."

His soft command had my heart palpitating and my pussy thumping. One thing about Gage was that he knew how much I loved being handled.

I pulled back, staring up at him. There was an

expectant yet playful spark in his eyes. My gaze stayed locked on his as I made my way to my knees. He watched me through lust-hazed eyes as I undid his pants and pulled them and his boxers down. His dick, long and thick, bobbed in front of me. Gage was working with a monster, and I knew my jaw and throat were about to take a beating but fuck it, I was ready for it.

I grabbed the base of his dick and ran my tongue up the length of it. The deep groan that filled the quiet of Gage's condo rumbled through my body, making me shiver. A pearl of pre-cum sat at the eye of his dick, and I swiped my tongue across it, lapping up the sticky sweetness. Gage ate really healthy - a lot of fruits and vegetables, and he tasted like it. I opened my mouth, ready to devour him whole, but he placed a hand on my shoulder, stilling me.

"You forgetting something," he said and lifted the container of sauce.

I watched as he removed the lid and poured a good amount onto his shaft. I ran my tongue across my lips and could almost taste the basil and other herbs. I couldn't wait to feel the weight of him on my tongue and what his taste mixed with the pizza sauce would be.

I dove right in, licking and sucking at the bright red sauce, making sure to get every drop. My taste buds were on overload as I licked Gage clean. The tangy sweetness of the sauce and the slightly salty taste of Gage were heady and made me want to devour him. Opening my mouth wide, I took him in and didn't stop until the tip of his dick was pressed against the back of my throat.

"Shit, Vanessa!" Gage groaned and latched onto a fistful of my hair.

I moaned around his dick and started bobby my head, moving up and down his shaft. I twirled my tongue and hallowed out my cheeks, trying to suck the life out of him.

"Fuck!" He roared and dug his fingers into my scalp. He used the grip he had on my hair to hold me in place while he fucked my mouth. His thrusts were hard, fast, and deep. My mouth only got wetter as he rammed himself down my throat.

My vision blurred as I gagged on him. Tears crested the corners of my eyes and trailed down my cheeks. Saliva dripped from the corners of my mouth and down my chin.

"Shit, V. You know I love that gagging shit. Umm-hmm...that's right. Take this fucking dick, baby girl," Gage gritted out.

I couldn't stop the moans escaping me or the way my body twisted and gyrated as I rubbed my thighs together, trying to get some friction against my throbbing clit.

Gage fucked my throat the same way he fucked my pussy, and I loved it. Even if my mascara was running down my face from the way my eyes watered. The harder he thrust, the wetter I got. I reached up and caressed his balls, kneading and stroking them. Gage hissed, and his body jerked in response.

"You tryna make Daddy come? You want this nut down your throat, V? Huh?" Gage talked shit as he continued to assault my mouth.

I moaned around his dick and nodded my head as best I could. I wanted him to come down my throat.

"Ah, shit!" Gage yelled as his grip on my hair tightened.

He was about to come.

I stared up at him through my lashes, wanting to see his sex faces. His brow was dipped in concentration, his pupils were blown with lust, and he had his bottom lip trapped between his teeth. He looked absolutely feral.

"You want this nut, baby girl?" He gritted out.

"Mmm-hmm," I moaned around his dick.

Gage sped up, his thrusts coming in faster and harder. After a minute, his movements became jerky as his orgasm came crashing down. "Fuck!" He bellowed as he pumped his cum down my throat.

I swallowed it down, loving the sweet taste of him.

"Fuck, V," Gage said as he released my hair and stumbled back.

I stayed on my knees, staring up at him, chest heaving, as I caught my breath.

Gage reached out and traced a finger through the trail of tears on my cheek, then across my swollen lips. "Come here," he softly commanded and helped me off the floor.

His eyes, dark and intense, bore into me. "Arms up," he commanded and helped me out of my shirt. His eyes stayed connected with mine as he unfastened my jeans and pulled them off. My heels had come off sometime while I was giving him head. "Let's shower," he said, then grabbed my hand and led me to the bathroom in his master suite.

Gage turned on the shower, removed the rest of his clothes, and then stripped me of my bra and panties. We stepped into the large shower. It was big enough to fit at least four people. It had dual rainshower heads with three body sprays. I loved his shower. It was perfect for showering together.

Gage squirted body wash onto a cloth and began washing my body. He ran the soft cloth over my arms, breasts, and torso, then down the front of my legs before having me turn around so he could wash my backside. I reciprocated by washing him in turn. Water and suds sluiced down his muscular frame, making him look like a glistening Egyptian God. I dropped the washcloth and ran my palms over his abs and down to his dick, which was covered in soap and standing at attention. I cupped my hands, gathering water from the shower, and poured it over his dick, washing the soap away before grabbing him at the base and squeezing. I reared up on my toes and ran my tongue across his lips. Gage caught me around the waist and pulled me against him. He opened his mouth and grabbed my tongue, pulling it into his mouth and sucking. I shivered at the velvety feel of his tongue against mine. My pussy, still slick from our encounter a few minutes ago, leaked even more. I could feel my juices running down my thighs and mingling with the shower water. I stroked Gage's shaft, squeezing lightly and eliciting a groan from him.

Gage braced his hands on my hips and guided me toward the shower wall. My back hit the cold tile, causing me to moan. Gage ate up my moan, licking and gently biting my lips and sucking on my tongue. He brought a hand to my pussy and dipped two fingers inside, stretching me. He worked his fingers in and out of my slick hole, tapping that sweet spot at the front of my pussy every time. He played in my pussy so good; I was coming in seconds.

"Gage," I whimpered as I came all over his fingers.

I watched as he brought those same fingers to his mouth and sucked.

"You taste so fucking good, V. Taste," he said and grabbed the back of my neck with his other hand. He kissed me, pressing his tongue into my mouth and swirling it around mine. The sweet taste of me on his tongue had my nipples beading and my pussy quivering.

"Lift your leg," Gage whispered against my lips.

I lifted my leg, and Gage hooked it around his waist. He gripped my thigh and then thrust up into me, stretching and filling my pussy with his girth.

"Shit, Gage!" I wailed into his mouth.

He started moving, and at this angle, I could feel every inch of him pushing, slapping, and stretching my walls. My back slammed into the shower wall with every hard plunge of his dick into my body. This shit was painful and would surely leave bruises, but the pleasure he was giving me was so much more that it trumped the pain. In fact, the pain almost heightened the pleasure.

"Turn around," Gage ordered as he slipped out of me and spun me around so I was facing the wall. He gripped my hips and slammed into me from behind. My damn knees almost buckled.

"Fuck!" I screamed as Gage started fucking me hard from behind. Over and over, he slammed into me; the sounds of our skin slapping and water sloshing filled the bathroom. "G-Gage! Oh God! Gage... please," I begged.

He wrapped a hand around my throat, forcing my head to tilt back so I could look up at him.

"Please what, V? Tell Daddy what you need," Gage gritted against my ear.

"I-I need...I need to come. Please," I whined.

Gage licked up the side of my neck to my ear, then said, "I got you, baby girl."

Gage tightened his grip on my neck, making it harder to breathe and, at the same time, causing chills to break out all over my body. He leveraged his hand at my waist to slam me back and forth on this dick. The force of his thrusts rocked me, and I cried out, moaning and screaming his name. The shit felt so good. My body was a livewire, and I was about to explode. I could feel my pussy tighten around him as my body quaked. He slid his hand from my waist to my pussy and pinched my clit. My body seized as my orgasm came crashing down.

"Shit! Fuck yeah! Give me all that nut, baby girl. This pussy so damn good. I'm bout to fucking... " Gage's words were lost as he came, filling me to the brim with his cum.

CHAPTER EIGHT

VINCE

The predawn chill wrapped around me as I stepped onto the private airstrip, the first light of morning casting long shadows across the tarmac. Dressed in tactical gear, every piece felt like an extension of myself. This wasn't just another assignment; it was my first major mission since joining the S & T Security Firm.

I glanced over at Sigma and the rest of our team, five seasoned operatives who had seen more action than most could claim in a lifetime. Despite the early hour, everyone was alert, the shared understanding of the mission's importance evident in their focused expressions.

My thoughts briefly flickered to Vanessa and our dinner date the other night, her laughter echoing in my mind—a stark contrast to the silence of the dawn. I allowed myself that brief moment, acknowledging the depth of what I felt for her. It wasn't a distraction but a reminder of what I had waiting for me, a reason to come back. I knew this job would be dangerous, and the thought of seeing her when it was all done would be in the back of my mind.

Sigma approached, his presence commanding yet familiar. The brief squeeze on my shoulder wasn't a gesture of reassurance but mutual respect between warriors. "You ready?" he asked, his voice carrying the weight of experiences and unspoken stories.

I nodded, meeting his eyes. "Yeah. Let's do it," I replied.

Sigma's smile was brief but genuine. "I know it's your first field assignment with us, and we don't do things in the traditional sense, but we get the job done quickly and quietly. You may see some things you ain't used to, but you'll be fine. We wouldn't have brought you on if you weren't up for it. Get through this first assignment, and the rest will be a piece of cake."

His words, simple yet powerful, bolstered my confidence. Not that I wasn't confident anyway. I knew who I was and what I could do. I'm good with my shit. At the same time, the pep talk was appreciated.

As we boarded the sleek, black jet that would take us to our destination, I took one last look at the slowly brightening sky. Today was about more than just a mission; it was about proving to myself that the path I'd chosen was where I was meant to be.

Settled in my seat, the roar of the engines pounded in my ears, the vibration through the cabin a call to arms. My mind ran over the mission details one last time, each element scrutinized and each outcome anticipated.

As the jet lifted off, slicing through the cool morning air, I allowed myself one final thought of Vanessa before homing my focus totally on the mission at hand.

We landed at an airstrip in the middle of nowhere and quickly unloaded our gear. Sigma led us to the only building in the remote area. From the outside, it looked like an old industrial warehouse, but once inside, it was clear that this was one of Sigma and Trace's facilities.

The walls, weathered and marked by time, stood as silent sentinels of the building's industrial history. Dim overhead lights cast eerie shadows across the vast expanse, creating an atmosphere of anticipation.

In one corner, a row of computer stations hummed with activity. Skilled technicians, bathed in the bluish glow of multiple screens, furiously typing away, monitoring crucial data and communication channels. Nearby, a makeshift command center had been set up, and along the wall were monitors with various map views of the location where Dijana was being held. Key routes and rooms inside the location were marked off.

"Hey, boss," a woman standing at a solid 5'9" greeted Sigma.

"What up, E. This is Vince. He's leading the extraction team with me today. Vince, this is Evangeline-"

"Governments? Is that what we doing now,

Sayid?" Evangeline hissed.

Sigma laughed. "Damn, E. I'm just messin' with you." He looked over at me. "That government name be having her hot. Let me start this introduction over before she cracks one of my ribs."

I looked at E., taking her in. Her raven-black hair was cropped short and framed a face that carried the subtle scars of battles fought and won. Her piercing, steely onyx eyes were like windows to a well-guarded inner world, hinting at the depths of her experience. Her body was lean and powerful - all muscle and she sported a faint scar that traced a path from her left eyebrow down to her chin. She clearly leaned into her masculinity, but there was a femininity to her that could not be denied. It was there in the softness of her chin, the roundness of her hips, and the intelligence in her gaze. Still, there was something deadly about her. There was no doubt in my mind that she could easily crack a guy's ribs or worse.

"Fuck you, Sig. I'll introduce myself," E said, then turned her black gaze on me. She eyed me assessingly, and the slight tip of the corner of her mouth told me she approved of what she saw. "Good to finally meet you, Vince. I've heard a lot about you."

"Good to meet you as well, E," I told her.

She nodded and then waved for us to follow her to the command center. "We've got eyes on all entrances above and below ground. They're holding more than just the girl in this location. This seems to be a regular holding spot for the girls they traffic. I know we want to get in and get out but with your permission, I'd like a team on standby to go in after you all extract the girl and get the rest of the girls out of there."

"Absolutely," Sigma quickly agreed. "I was going to talk to you about that anyway. You got a team together already?"

"I do," E replied.

"Then do it. You got my go-ahead. We're heading straight from the compound to the airport after we get the girl but hit me up after, and we'll debrief," Sigma said.

We spent the next couple of hours studying the location and going over our entry and exit points, positions, and timing. We needed to be swift and precise.

As the day faded into night, we loaded up and headed to the location.

Under the cloak of night, our team approached the compound, a sprawling fortress of concrete and steel nestled deep in a heavily wooded area. The air was thick with tension, every shadow a potential threat, every sound a possible alarm. It was here, in the suffocating silence of anticipation, that Sigma transformed from the charismatic leader into a commander sculpted by years of what I figured to be covert operations. I could only guess because he never talked about his past.

I watched Sigma closely. I was confident in my

skills, but this wasn't his first rodeo. He was in his element. There was a fluidity to his movements, a certainty in his commands that spoke of countless nights just like this one. He seemed to come alive in the shadow of danger, his calm demeanor a stark contrast to the lethal decisiveness of how he approaches missions.

The compound loomed before us, a monolith of darkness against the starless sky. Sigma surveyed the scene with a critical eye. "Vince, Ace, you're with me. We'll take the north side. The rest of the team will circle around and create a diversion on the west. We hit them in five."

His orders were met with silent nods, the team dispersing without a sound. I felt a surge of adrenaline as I followed Sigma, the weight of my gear a comforting presence against my back.

As we neared the compound, Sigma's hand on my shoulder was a grounding force. "Stay alert," he muttered, his focus unwavering.

As we slipped through the compound's defenses, the silence was almost suffocating, broken only by the faint hum of machinery. Our footsteps were muted, our breathing controlled as we navigated the dimly lit corridors. Sigma led us through the shadows, every step calculated, every breath measured. The entrance we chose had the least amount of guards, and hell, Sigma neutralized half of them before I blinked. The man was lethal, quietly slicing through the necks of three of the five guards in under two seconds.

Before the other two guards could draw their weapons, Ace snapped the necks of both men. He did it so fast that I almost missed it.

We continued quickly and quietly toward our target. Meanwhile, chaos erupted on the west side of the compound as the diversion team did their part, drawing the bulk of the guards to that side of the compound.

As we moved, the world narrowed to the corridor before us, Sigma at the lead, his gun an extension of his will. We moved as one, a unit bound by a singular purpose – to rescue Dijana and bring her home.

Turning a corner, Sigma signaled a halt, his hand raised. Ahead, the faint murmur of voices indicated we were not alone. With a series of hand gestures, he outlined the plan – Ace would take the lead, I would follow, and Sigma would cover our exit. There was no room for error, every movement had to be precise, deliberate.

We advanced, the voices growing louder. We came upon two men, dressed in black standing guard in front of a heavy metal door. Ace had a bullet in each man's head before they even realized what happened. We moved quickly and quietly to the door. Ace got to work, his tools silent as shadows as he bypassed the lock. The door swung open silently on well-oiled hinges, revealing a dimly lit room beyond.

Inside, Dijana sat on a cold concrete floor, her knees drawn up to her chest. Her blue eyes, wide with fear, flicked up to us, taking in our tactical gear, the weapons in our hands. For a moment, she recoiled, fear etching deeper lines into her pale face.

"It's okay. We're here to take you home. Your father sent us," Sigma said, his voice a calm anchor in the storm of her fear. He stepped forward, lowering his weapon, his hands held out in a gesture of peace.

Dijana hesitated, then, as if the reality of her rescue sank in, relief washed over her face in waves. She scrambled to her feet, moving towards us with a newfound urgency.

"We need to move, now," Sigma said, his voice low. The sounds of the diversion were beginning to fade, our window of escape narrowing with each passing second.

We moved back through the corridors, Sigma in the lead, Dijana between us, and Ace covering our six. Every shadow and every sound had us tensing, ready for confrontation. But the team's planning had been meticulous; the route was clear, and our escape seemingly unnoticed.

As we continued through the shadowed maze of the compound, our escape was almost too smooth. My instincts, honed from years on the force, screamed that it wouldn't last. And it didn't.

A sudden burst of movement to our right had me pivoting on instinct, just as a guard emerged from the darkness, his weapon raised and pointing at Sigma. Time seemed to slow as our eyes met. In that split second, I saw no option, but hesitation wasn't a luxury I could afford.

Without a second thought, I lunged forward, tackling the guard to the ground. His training was evident, but desperation lent me an edge. Our struggle was silent but brutal. He landed a few blows to my ribs before I was able to subdue him with my hunting knife to the side of his neck. He gurgled as blood spilled from the wound.

My heart pounded as I released him and scrambled to my feet. I'd had to end a life before when I was an officer, but never like this - never this close-up on some hand-to-hand combat shit. It was a little unnerving. The brief encounter with the guard, a moment of life and death, was a stark reminder of the cost of our work. My actions, driven by instinct and the will to protect, left a mark on my soul, a reminder of the fragility of life.

As I stood over the dying man, Sigma's voice broke through the quiet. "You did what needed to be done," he said, his voice low and steady. His gaze held mine for a moment, a shared understanding of the cost of our line of work.

We moved quickly after that, the sound of the helicopter growing louder as we neared the extraction point. Reaching the exterior, the cool night air hit us like a wave, the open sky a stark contrast to the claustrophobia of the compound. Sigma led us to a pre-arranged extraction point, a shadowed area where the terrain provided cover and an escape route.

The sound of rotors cut through the night as a helicopter descended, its presence a promise of safety. Sigma ushered Dijana aboard first, then followed, his gaze scanning the horizon for any sign of pursuit. Ace and I boarded last, the doors shutting with a finality that marked the end of the rescue.

As the helicopter lifted off, Dijana, now safe within its confines, allowed herself to collapse, her relief palpable. Sigma sat beside her, offering quiet reassurances, his demeanor shifting from commander to protector.

I watched the compound recede below us. The disdain I had for a place like that was only quelled by the knowledge that E would be sending in a team to rescue the rest of the young women and demolish the place. Had I been on the force still, it would have taken us months to get approval to even put eyes on the place. Working with Sigma and Trace meant no red tape, which meant we could help more people faster.

As I settled into my seat, my adrenaline was still pumping from taking that guard down. He put up a good fight, and I was lucky to have only a few injuries. My thoughts immediately went to Vanessa. The idea of being hurt and not being able to see her or touch her didn't sit well with me, and the need to see her right away became a tangible ache for me. I realized that she was my anchor, the one constant in a world that was becoming increasingly murky.

CHAPTER NINE

VANESSA

The morning sun cast a golden hue over Eastbrook's quaint streets as Gabby and I strolled from one potential wedding venue to the next. Each place had its charm, but my mind was a whirlwind of emotions, making it hard to focus on the task at hand.

"I like the garden setting of this one, but the ballroom in the first place was breathtaking," Gabby mused, her eyes sparkling with excitement.

I nodded, trying to match her enthusiasm. "Yeah, the ballroom had a great vibe. Very... elegant."

Gabby glanced at me, her expression turning thoughtful. "You're not really here, are you? What's going on, V?"

I sighed, the facade crumbling. "You already know. The same thing that's been plaguing me since your engagement party. Gage and Vince... I still have no idea what to do, Gabby. I just... I don't know. My feelings for both of them only continue to grow. I love the way I feel when I'm with them, and I don't want to lose that. Choosing one of them means losing half of what makes me happy."

Gabby stopped walking, pulling me to a bench nearby. "I been thinking about your dilemma."

I chuckled. "Oh, have you now?"

Gabby's eyes narrowed, and she pursed her lips. "Do you want my advice or not?" She asked.

I rolled my eyes dramatically and nodded. "Lay it on me."

"Don't choose," she offered, and I went to protest, but she put a hand up, stopping me. "Just hear me out. You clearly have strong feelings for both men, and they clearly have the same feelings for you. And let's be honest, they have to know about each other on some level. I mean, they've both seen you interact with the other. It's clear that you don't want to give either of them up, and based on my observation of how they are with you, I don't think either man wants to lose you either."

Gabby's words hung in the air between us, sparking a whirlwind of thoughts. I found myself reflecting on the moments that had defined my connections with each man. With Gage, it was his playfulness, his charm, and the way my heart seemed to dance when he was near. His energy was infectious, a constant source of joy and excitement that made every day brighter. And I can't leave out his sex game because, phew, child!

And then there was Vince, whose presence was like a calm harbor in the midst of a storm. With him, I found peace and a sense of security I hadn't known I was seeking. His strength wasn't just physical but emotional too. And the way he made love to my body was something of romance novels. He was slow and deliberate, leaving no parts of my body untouched.

Each man offered something essential, something that made me feel whole in different ways. It wasn't about comparing them or measuring one against the other. It was about recognizing that my heart had the capacity to hold them both, each in their own right. I knew that was what Gabby was getting at, but still, how could I just not choose?

"Wouldn't that be unfair, not choosing?" I questioned.

Gabby took my hand, her gaze sincere. "Maybe it's not about fairness in the conventional sense. Maybe it's about being true to yourself and honest with them. And hell, they might surprise you."

Her advice, while daunting, ignited a flicker of hope within me. Perhaps there was a way to navigate this, to be true to my feelings without losing a part of myself in the process.

I made it home a little after 6pm. Venue hunting turned out to be successful as Gabby ended up choosing the Historic Eastbrook Mansion as her venue. My girl's wedding was coming together nicely, and I couldn't be happier for her.

I ordered dinner from my favorite Chinese

restaurant, then shed my clothes as I made my way to my en suite bathroom to take a quick shower. I let the warm water cascade over my body for a minute, then squirted some lavender soap onto a washcloth and washed the day away. I stepped out of the shower feeling refreshed. I quickly dried off, oiled my body, and put on one of my favorite lounge sets. By the time I made it to the living room, my Chinese food was at the door.

I spread my food out on the coffee table, turned on one of my favorite K-Dramas, and dug into my food.

About thirty minutes in, the soft hum of an engine could be heard from my driveway. I checked my phone to see if I had any missed calls or messages. There were none, so who the hell had pulled up unannounced?

I made my way to the window and peeked out to see Vince climbing out of his truck. My stomach fluttered at the sight of him. He looked so damn good in a pair of dark jeans and a polo.

I hurried to the door, fluffing my curls out a bit, and pulled it open. Before I could even register his presence fully, Vince was on me. His arms wrapped around me in a fierce embrace, pulling me against his solid, muscular frame. There was an urgency in his touch and a hunger in his eyes that sent a wave of heat coursing through me. Without a word, Vince wrapped his hand around my throat, pulling me toward him. The move was aggressive and unexpected from him, but damn if it didn't make my pussy clench.

Vince's lips crashed against mine in a kiss that was both desperate and deeply passionate. I melted into him, the world around us fading into a blur. His hands roamed my body, leaving trails of fire in their wake. He lifted me effortlessly, pressing me against the front door as he kissed me, his body molding perfectly to mine. It was as if he was trying to convey everything he couldn't put into words through his touch.

The intensity of our connection at that moment was overwhelming, a tangible expression of the emotions that had been building in his absence. Vince's usual calm and composed demeanor was replaced by a raw, primal need that matched my own. I wrapped my legs around his waist, pulling him closer, needing to feel every inch of him against me.

Our tongues connected as he hummed, a deep, gravelly rumble that had my knees weak and my panties soaked. I ground my center into him, needing the friction. I could feel how hard his dick was through his jeans, and it excited me even more.

Vince pulled back from the kiss, and I took in some much-needed air. His normally warm eyes were dark and intense as he stared at me. There was an urgency in them as he slid my pants and panties down my legs in one fell swoop. I bit down on my lip as I watched him quickly undo his pants and free his dick. It was a thing of beauty. It was long, at least eight inches, thick as shit, and hooked nicely to the left. My pussy literally pulsed in anticipation.

Without saying a word, Vince pushed me back against the door and did a quick swipe of his fingers between my folds, smearing my juices around. He lifted one of my legs, hooked it around his waist, and then drove into me with a force that had me shivering and crying out.

Before I could get my bearings, Vince was slamming into me, and I had to brace my arms around his neck for some semblance of stability. Vince was on one as he pounded away at my pussy, and my girl loved it. She was soaked and weeping so much that wet sounds reverberated through the room every time Vince entered and exited my pussy.

Vince was punishing my girl, my backside slamming against the door with every thrust. He was feral, and his heavy grunts played in my ear like an old-school love song, and I needed that shit on replay.

"Fuck, Vince! Fuck!" I moaned as he pounded into me. That curve was serving its purpose in this position as his tip repeatedly tapped against the sensitive spot in my pussy. "V-Vince...I'm going...I'm going to..." My words were cut off as my body tensed with overwhelming pleasure. My orgasm hit so hard and fast that I screamed, my nails digging into his shoulders and my thighs clenching around his waist.

Vince followed me right over the edge, his body tensing and his dick flinching inside me as he came on a roar. The grip he had on my thigh tightened as he pressed himself deeper into me, almost like he was trying to meld us together. It made me feel safe and desired.

We stayed that way, locked together, for a few minutes before finally coming down from the high of our fervent reunion. Without a word, Vince carried me to the bedroom, his movements slow and deliberate. He removed my top, quickly shed the rest of his clothes, then laid me on the bed and made love to me in his usual way - slow, methodical, and intense, each movement a testament to the depth of what he felt for me.

He started at my toes, kissing and sucking each one before trailing his lips along the skin of my shins up to my thighs. I squirmed as he drew circles with his tongue on my inner thigh. I knew where he was heading, and my core pulsed and leaked in anticipation.

Vince was a man of little words during sex. He preferred to let his mouth, hands, and dick to the talking, and they haven't disappointed yet.

I stared down at Vince between my legs and watched with anticipation as he swiped his tongue up my soaked slit, tasting me and his own essence in the process. The shit was so sexy. I reached down and ran my hands through his kinky curls as he lapped and sucked on my clit.

Vince was feasting on me, and I felt like I was detaching from reality. The way he sucked and pulled on my little nub had me thrashing and moaning. And when he thrust his tongue inside and flicked it against my G-spot, I lost it. "Vince!" I screamed as my orgasm hit. My body shook, and I dug my fingers into his scalp. White dots were all I saw as my essence flooded his mouth, and Vince groaned as he slurped up every drop.

After having his fill, he kissed his way up my body and settled between my thighs. "Missed you," was all he said before taking my mouth and kissing me deeply as he slowly slid himself inside me.

"Mmm...shit," I moaned. No matter how many times we fucked, that first breach always did something to me.

Vince placed kisses on my face, neck, and breast as he fucked me slowly and deeply. It was like he was trying to reach into the very depths of my being. We always connected on some level during sex, but this was something else. It was like he was infiltrating every part of me.

Mind.

Body.

Soul.

I felt him in the very essence of who I was, and that kicked off the start of my second orgasm.

"Mmm...you bout to come, love?" Vince whispered against my neck.

I moaned and stretched, giving him more access to my throat. "Yes," I breathed out.

"Well, let's come together," Vince said, then grabbed my leg and pushed it up to my chest, leaving me wide open to his assault of my pussy.

His movements sped up a bit, but he was still giving me those deep, hard thrusts. With every stroke, he pulled out of me to the tip and then rocked back into me so hard that my body shifted upward. He did this repeatedly. Hell, he did it until I was writing, moaning, and coming all over him.

"Gawtdamn, Vince! So good...so so fucking...good!" I wailed.

Vince caught my mouth, kissing me deeply as his own body began to jerk. He pounded into me, riding me through my orgasm and his own.

After taking care of our hygiene, we lay in bed, Vince's arms wrapped tightly around me. I could sense a weight on Vince's mind. He was unusually quiet, his gaze distant. Not to mention how he'd just rolled up on me, no phone call or text, something he never did. And the way he fucked me against the door, rushed and wild, that was different for him. Something was bothering my guy. "Vince?" I whispered, tracing patterns on his chest. "You good? You seem a little..." I let the words die on my lips because I didn't want to lead him in the conversation.

He let out a deep sigh, the sound heavy with unspoken burdens. "Yeah... I just...my first assignment. It was... intense. A girl was taken. They were going to traffic her. We rescued her, but..." His voice trailed off, the unspoken words hanging in the air between us.

I propped myself up on my elbow, looking into his eyes. "But what? You know you can talk to me about anything."

He turned to face me; his eyes dark with a turmoil I had never seen before. "I had to... take down one of the guards. It was him or us. I've been in tough spots before, but this... it was different."

I could hear the conflict in his voice, the struggle to reconcile the necessity of his actions with the cost they carried. I reached up, cupping his face in my hands. "You did what needed to be done, Vince. You saved that girl's life."

He closed his eyes, leaning into my touch. "I know, but it's a lot to take in. V, this was some hand-to-hand combat type shit. I could have easily..." his voice trailed off.

"What? You could have easily what, Vince?" I

probed.

"Died. I could have died. He was a big dude, and he could hold his own."

"Yeah, but Sigma was there, right? He wouldn't let anything happen to you."

"He was right there, and I knew he would have stepped in if necessary. It's not really that."

I gently ran my thumb back and forth across his cheek. "Then what is it?"

"It was my first up-close kill. That shit hits differently, you know?" He said.

I couldn't even begin to imagine the emotions he was going through, but I could comfort him. I pulled him into a gentle embrace. "You're one of the toughest, smartest, most thoughtful men I know. You'll work through this. If this job is for you, you'll stay. If not, you'll go. Either way, I'll be around to support you. I got you."

CHAPTER TEN

VANESSA

The first light of dawn crept through the curtains, casting a soft glow across the room, touching scattered clothes and the disheveled sheets—a testament to the night before. The apartment was silent, save for the soft, rhythmic ticking of the old-school alarm clock on my nightstand and my own steady breathing. I lay there, wrapped in a blanket, alone, Vince's presence lingering like a warm shadow.

Last night with Vince was... indescribable. The urgency in his touch, the desperation in our connection. It was as if, in those moments, he was affirming something profound between us, something beyond words. It was like he was trying to imprint himself onto my very soul. And then there was the gentle aftermath, the way he made love to me with such tenderness, each movement deliberate, as if worshiping every inch of me. And Vince's vulnerability last night, the way he opened up about the mission, about the life he had to take—it fucked with him and I felt that. In his confession, in the weight of his gaze, I saw a glimpse of the depth of his emotions, of the man behind the calm facade. It was a connection that felt as deep and as vast as the ocean, a bond that seemed to tether me to him in ways I was only beginning to understand.

It was a contrast to the fiery, dominating, and passionate connection I shared with Gage, who had the unique ability to draw me out, to make me forget the complexities of life, and just live in the joy of the moment. Being with him felt like coming up for air, like finding a piece of myself I didn't even know was missing.

And don't get me started on their sex game. They handled me very differently in the bedroom, and I needed what both of them offered. But it wasn't just the pussy shattering sex. I craved what they gave me sexually, but I needed what they gave me mentally and emotionally.

The realization that my feelings for both men were not just lingering but had grown stronger was crazy. Crazy, like, I think I was in love with both of them crazy. But how could that be? How could I love them both so completely yet so differently? Was it even possible to sustain this, to keep bouncing between two halves of a whole, without eventually having to choose?

The thought of choosing, of losing one to keep the other, tightened something in my chest. It felt like choosing between breathing and my heartbeat - both essential to my very existence. Gabby's words echoed in my mind, suggesting maybe I didn't have to choose in the traditional sense. But the idea of a polyamorous relationship, of being open and honest with both Vince and Gage, was wild. How would they react? Could they understand the depth of my feelings for them both?

I rose from the bed, the chill of the floor a sharp contrast to the warmth of the blankets. Wrapping a robe around me, I moved to the window, watching as the city slowly woke. The idea of exploring a polyamorous relationship was foreign, intriguing, and terrifying all at once. And was I even brave enough to broach the subject with Vince and Gage?

Steeling myself, I turned from the window, the morning light now fully spilling into the room. I grabbed my laptop out of my bag and got back in bed. Placing my laptop on my thighs, I settled back against the pillows piled against the headboard. The soft morning light spilled over the keyboard as I hesitated for a moment, the cursor blinking in the search bar. Typing "polyamorous relationships" felt like stepping into uncharted territory, a world I knew existed but never in life thought I'd be exploring.

As I hit enter, the screen flooded with articles, forums, and personal stories. Each click took me deeper into the experiences of others who loved more than one person and who navigated the complexities of multiple relationships with honesty and consent. I read about the challenges, the jealousy that sometimes arose, and the communication required to maintain such relationships. But there was also talk of immense fulfillment, of love amplified rather than divided, of partnerships strengthened by openness and trust.

I found myself drawn to a blog by someone who lived in a successful polyamorous relationship. They wrote about the initial fears and misunderstandings, about the societal judgments they faced, and about the deep, unwavering love they shared with their partners. It was eye-opening, the way they described polyamory not as a limitation but as an expansion of their capacity to love and be loved.

Yet, with every story of success, there were accounts of struggles, hard conversations, and the need for boundaries and agreements. It wasn't a solution devoid of complications; it was a choice that demanded continual effort and adaptation.

The more I read, the more I realized how little I knew about polyamory beyond the surface. It wasn't just about loving more than one person; it was about building relationships with honesty, respect, and communication at their core. It was about knowing yourself, your needs, and your boundaries and sharing those openly with those you love.

Feeling overwhelmed, I closed the laptop and sat there in silence, absorbing everything I had learned. The curiosity that had driven my search was now mixed with a whirlwind of confusion and introspection. The only thing that I could think of to help me through this was coffee and my bestie. I picked up my phone and texted Gabby.

Me: I need some coffee and my bestie. Sips-N-Kicks?
Bestie: Griff made breakfast. We have gourmet coffee. Come to the penthouse.
Me: Oh! You got that nigga so sprung that he cooking and stocking up on gourmet coffee. That va-jay-jay of yours is a beast! lol!
Bestie: ROFL! I can't stand you!
Me: Love you too. See you in about 30.

My beloved city of Eastbrook was bathed in the soft glow of the morning sun as I made my way to Gabby and Griff's penthouse. My heart was heavy with thoughts and emotions, but the promise of clarity, or at least the comfort of sharing my burden with my bestie, lightened my steps.

I used the key Gabby gave me to let myself in and was immediately met with the aroma of freshly brewed gourmet coffee and something sweet.

Gabby greeted me with a warm hug and a knowing look in her eyes. "Griff made your favorite, blueberry lemon pancakes," she said, leading me to the kitchen where Griff was putting the final touches on a spread that looked like it belonged in a five-star restaurant.

"Morning, Vanessa," Griff greeted me with a smile, passing me a cup of coffee that smelled like heaven.

I stared down into the mug and grinned. "Hold up. Is this what I think it is?" I looked at Griff. "Bruh-in-law! Tell me you didn't make me an apple crisp macchiato?"

Griff laughed and nodded. "Thank ya girl! She had me go out and grab the stuff when you told her you were coming over."

My eyes softened as I looked at Griff. "I'm always grateful for my bestie because I know she gon' look out no matter what, but for you to go out and get the ingredients and make it for me..." I set my mug on the counter, walked over to Griff, and threw my arms around his neck. "You a good goddamn man, Griffin Thayer. Me and my bestie are lucky to have you."

Griff shook his head as he hugged me back. "You crazy as hell. You know that, right?"

I sucked my teeth and lifted a brow as I looked up at him. "Oh, I'm aware. The real question is, you know you ain't never getting out, right?" I half-joked as I released him and grabbed my mug.

Griff's chest rumbled as he chuckled. "That's fine with me. Trust. Your bestie got me on lock, which is exactly where I wanna be. Now, let's eat. Food's ready," Griff said.

We settled at the breakfast bar to eat, the penthouse windows offering a breathtaking view of Eastbrook. The food was delicious, but it was the company and the conversation that nourished me more.

After some small talk, I dove into the heart of

why I was there. "So, Gabs, I been thinking about what you said the other day about the guys and me, and it's really been on my mind, especially having seen them both rather recently. And look, I want to take your advice, but if I'm honest, I'm scared."

Gabby's brow lifted, and I knew it was because being scared is something I've never admitted to. But that's because not much scares me.

"So, I did some research... about polyamory," I started, then shared my thoughts, fears about what people would think, and the insights I'd gained from my research. Gabby listened intently and didn't speak until I was done.

"I think it's great that you looked into the lifestyle. You've always juggled men but what you have with Griff and Vince is way more serious than any other entanglements you've been in. And the way you three are, a poly relationship might work for ya'll. And I still maintain that honesty and transparency are the best paths."

Griff, who had been quietly listening, finally spoke. "Gage and Vince are both my boys, and you like a sister to me, V. I want all of ya'll to be happy. I've seen how Vince and Gage handle you. It's clear they both care about you deeply. Hell, if I'm honest, as long as I've known Gage, he's never simped behind a woman the way he does for you-"

My eyes rounded, and my jaw dropped. "Simp? You think Gage simps for me?"

Griff chortled. "You know that's a term niggas

like to use to joke on boys, but you know what I mean. My nigga is down bad for you. Hell, he has a multi-million-dollar home in Atlanta, yet he spends ninety percent of his time here in Eastbrook. Why you think that is?"

My response was quick. "He's training with you."

Griff's brow furrowed, and his head tilted slightly as he looked at me. "Yeah, but he's trained with folks before in their hometown and didn't buy a half-million-dollar condo there. He bought one here... cuz you're here." He paused to let that sink in, then continued. "As for Vince, I'm still getting to know dude, but anyone can see that ol' boy is smitten with you. And listening to you talk, you feel the same way about both of them. You just scared of what people will think. Maybe not worry about that shit and do what makes you happy."

Griff's words, simple yet profound, struck a chord with me. He and Gabby were right. Honesty was scary but necessary. "See, that's why I love y'all. You two be gettin' me right together."

Gabby and Griff both laughed.

"Seriously. Thank you for listening to me drone on and on about my love life." I fixed my gaze on Gabby. "And you especially. You've been letting me burn your ear up about this for a while now. I appreciate you so much, friend."

"Aww, V," Gabby said, opening her arms for a hug that I quickly walked into. "You know I got you. Whenever. For Whatever," she added.

"I know and ditto," I told her as I hugged her

tightly. "And I'll seriously think about talking to them. I just need to work up the nerve and figure out what to say."

Leaving the penthouse a little while later, my mind was a whirl of thoughts. I didn't even see Gage come through the door. I bumped right into him. His presence was like a jolt to my senses.

"Hey, gorgeous," Gage greeted, pulling me into his arms for a quick yet deeply affectionate kiss.

"Hey yourself," I replied, my heart fluttering at his touch.

"What you doing here? Come to see me?" Gage asked with a boyish grin.

I smiled up at him. "I'm always down to see you, but that's not why I'm here. I had breakfast with Gabby and Griff. Where you coming from?"

"Had an early morning meeting with my management team," he replied.

"Oh yeah? How'd it go?" I asked.

His brow furrowed slightly. "It was cool. Training's about to get intense, though. They want me completely focused, which means I won't have much free time these next few weeks leading up to the fight."

"That makes sense. Your fight's next month. We need you laser-focused on your training. I told you; I don't date losers."

Gage closed the small distance between us, wrapping an arm around my waist and pinning me against his big body. With his other hand, he cupped the back of my head, digging his fingers into my curls and holding my head in place. His gaze burned hot as he stared down at me. "You always got jokes. I'm serious, girl. We already don't get a lot of time, and now it's going to be even less time with you. And my manager likes for me to cut out all sex in the few weeks leading up to the fight. It never used to bother me, but I'm not sure I'mma be able to do that, not with yo sexy ass," he whispered against my lips.

I reared back and frowned up at him. "Like a total ban or..."

Disappointment showed in his gaze. "Total ban," he confirmed.

"Ugh! Seriously? I don't like that at all," I whined.

"Trust, I'm with you, sweetheart, but..." Gage let the sentence die on his lips. His very full and very enticing lips.

I reared up on my toes and pressed a soft kiss to his mouth. I pulled back and brushed a hand against his cheek. "It's definitely not ideal, but we need you in tip-top shape for the fight, and besides, you can make it up to me by bringing me a championship belt."

"I already own two belts-"

I cut him off. "Then win this upcoming fight and bring me your third belt."

Gage smiled like a kid in a candy store. "I got you," he told me as he kissed and nibbled on my mouth.

I surrendered easily, melting into him, and opening my mouth wide to give him full access, and he didn't disappoint. Gage devoured me, running his tongue across my gums, the roof of my mouth, and the insides of my cheeks before latching onto my tongue and sucking on it like his favorite treat. I wrapped my arms around him and ran my hands up his back as our tongues dueled.

"Aren't you supposed to be heading to the gym for our session?" Griff's voice floated across the lobby.

I tried to pull back, but Gage held me captive, pulling and sucking on my tongue until he had his fill. I was overheated, horny, and completely breathless when he finally pulled back. I looked sheepishly over at Griff.

"And ain't you supposed to be at work," Griff accused, but there was a glint of humor in his eyes.

"Don't worry about where mine is supposed to be," Gage barked, but there was no bite to it.

"Whatever. Just have yo ass at the gym on time," Griff said as he strolled to the door. "Later, Vanessa," he added smugly before going out the door.

I giggled as I buried my head in Gage's chest.

"That nigga get on my nerves, but he's right," Gage said. "I gotta change and head out, and you gotta get to work."

I let out a heavy sigh. I would rather go up to Gage's place and spend the morning having my back blown out, but Griff was right. We both had obligations. I slowly lifted my head to look up at Gage. "Guess I'll head to work then. Have a good workout, baby," I told Gage, then kissed him lightly on the chin. I went to pull away, but Gage caught me by the chin.

"You be good. And look, I know I'mma be outta pocket for a minute, but don't forget about ya boy," he said.

I searched his gaze as he stared down at me. The playfulness I loved was there, but there was also something unsaid in the depths of his eyes. I ran my thumb across his full lips, then cupped his jaw. "I could never forget about you, Gage. You're too much a part of me. Now go focus on your training so you win, and I can celebrate by wearing that third belt and nothing else."

I felt Gage's dick twitch against my stomach and grinned. I loved the effect I had on him. If I didn't leave now, I wouldn't be leaving for a good while because I'd be spread beneath Gage, getting my pussy pummeled. So, I lifted up on my toes, kissed him, and said, "Have a good workout, handsome."

Gage's kisses stayed with me as I headed to my office. His playfully loving greeting, the urgency of his kiss—it all felt incredibly right. The way he held me and kissed me spoke volumes. The connection we had was something else. I just loved how free and comfortable we were with each other. Yet, as he shared his upcoming absence due to training, even though I played it off, a pang of sadness hit me. I didn't want limited time with Gage. I wanted more time. More of him. I wanted more of his laughter and spontaneity and the way he wrapped me up in his big arms and held me close. And, of course, I wanted as many belly-tightening, pussy quivering, mind-blowing orgasms as he was willing to give. I wanted everything from Gage Emerson.

That thought quickly brought Vince to mind, and I thought about our connection. I lived for Vince's serene presence, the deep soul-stirring connection we shared, the feeling of being seen and understood on a level I hadn't known existed, and that his sex game was top-tier. The slow way he made love to my body and mind was something else. It was all those things that I loved about Vince - needed from Vince. These men were two halves of me, and I couldn't see myself being without either of them.

CHAPTER ELEVEN

VANESSA

The sun was just beginning to dip into the golden hours of the afternoon when Vince and I arrived at the private gun range he's a member of. I'd made jokes a few times about infiltrating his club and getting some of the nice men to show me how to shoot. His only response had been a low growl, but now here we were, heading into the gun range. The anticipation bubbling inside me was a mix of excitement and a smidge of nervousness. I talked a good game, but I'd never even held a gun before, and the thrill of trying something new, especially with Vince, had me hyped.

Vince, with his usual calm demeanor, glanced over at me, a hint of a smirk playing on his lips. "Ready to have some fun?" he asked, his voice laced with excitement that matched my own.

I nodded, feeling a rush of adrenaline just from the energy around us. "You know it," I replied, eager to step into this new experience with him.

The range was a sprawling complex, far more upscale than I had imagined. The interior was sleek and modern, with state-of-the-art equipment and an array of firearms displayed like museum pieces. Vince led me through the facility with a familiarity that spoke volumes of his expertise and comfort in this environment.

We were greeted by a range officer, a burly man with a stern face that softened when he saw Vince. "Vince! What up? Good to see you again," he boomed, offering his hand for a shake.

"Hey, what's up, Joe?" Vince greeted as he took the man's outstretched hand and shook it.

"Shit! Just tryna make a living. You know how it is," he said.

Vince nodded. "I hear that."

Joe turned his brown gaze on me. "And who is this, lovely young lady?"

"This is Vanessa," Vince introduced me, his hand finding its way to the small of my back. "It's her first time at a range."

Joe gave me a warm smile. "Nice to meet you, Vanessa. You're in good hands with this one." He pointed to Vince, then leaned in and whispered, "But hit me up if he gets out of hand, and I'll handle him for ya and then take you out for a nice dinner." Joe wiggled his eyebrows, and I burst out laughing.

I looked over at Vince, who was smirking and shaking his head. He pulled me away from Joe. "Quit flirting with my girl and tell us what room we're in, Old Man," Vince barked, but there was no bite to it.

Joe let out a hearty laugh. "Calm down, young buck. Ain't nobody tryna steal your lady. Unless she wants to be stolen," he added with a wink in my direction.

Vince let out a loud sigh and frowned. "Room number?"

Joe, still amused, grinned big. "I put you in room 4. Head on back before I really do steal your girl."

I cackled, and Vince just waved him off.

"Have fun you two," Joe said.

"Yeah. Yeah. Thanks for getting the room ready," Vince told Joe as he led me to the private room Joe had set up for us. The room was near the back of the building, offering a sense of privacy and intimacy that I hadn't expected. Vince began explaining the basics—safety protocols, how to hold a gun, stance, and aiming. His instructions were clear and patient, his hands guiding mine with a gentleness that contrasted the power of the weapon I was about to handle.

The first time I pulled the trigger, the recoil startled me, but Vince's steady presence behind me, his hands on my shoulder and waist, grounded me. "You good. Just stay calm and breathe," he encouraged, and with each subsequent shot, my confidence grew.

We spent the next hour experimenting with different firearms, Vince sharing tips and techniques, his pride evident whenever I hit the targets. The exhilaration of firing, the focus it demanded, it all washed away the noise of the outside world, leaving just Vince and me in our bubble of concentrated energy.

A few hours later, after having shot way too

many different weapons, Vince and I packed up. My hands were still trembling with leftover adrenaline, a wide grin plastered on my face. "That was so fucking fun, Vince," I breathed out, amazed at how much I had enjoyed the experience.

Vince looked over, his eyes softening as he took in my excited state. "I'm glad you liked it. I know guns get a bad rap, especially given the state of the world today, but if we could get our political leaders to do what they should and impose common-sense gun laws, we can start to mend things in our country. At least related to gun violence."

I nodded. He was right. Guns were a very contentious subject, and we definitely needed common sense laws nationwide. I must say, though, that I was proud of my little city of Eastbrook for the gun laws we have in place - background checks, a waiting period, and a safe storage law. "Agreed," I told Vince. "I'm just glad that Eastbrook is doing its part to protect its citizens."

He nodded and grabbed my hand, leading me to the door. "Me too. So, you clearly enjoyed today. Tell me what you liked about it."

"The shooting," I said with a laugh.

Vince smirked. "Yeah. There's something about shooting... it's empowering, isn't it?"

I nodded, leaning into his side as we made our way out. "It really is. Things were rocky at first, but once I got used to the kickback, I felt... alive. A little bit like a badass, if I'm honest."

He wrapped an arm around me, pulling me close. "You looked like an absolute badass," he praised before dipping his head and placing a soft kiss to my temple. "My little badass. We need to get you a gun anyway for your place. I'll enroll you in a gun safety class, and we can come here so you can practice shooting."

"I'm so down. I wish we would have done this before Gabby and I got kidnapped last year. It would have been nice to know how to handle a piece and have it at the ready. We may not have got kidnapped," I said.

"Maybe. Maybe not. You two were outmanned. But, either way, it's a good skillset to have," Vince said.

We left the gun range and headed to the Park District. Vince had packed a little picnic for us to enjoy under the stars.

The sun receded into the horizon, painting the sky with strokes of orange and pink as Vince and I arrived at Eastbrook's Park District. This was one of my favorite districts in Eastbrook, with its lush greenery, flower gardens, and gorgeous pond. It also housed me and Gabby's favorite coffee spot, Sips-N-Kicks. Vince had packed a picnic for us to have dinner in the park.

I cut my eyes over at Vince, walking next to me carrying the picnic basket and blankets. This man was something else. The day he planned for us was far from traditional, and I loved that. First, the gun range, and now this. Butterflies tickled my stomach, and I inhaled deeply in an effort to settle it.

We set up under a large tree not far from the pond. The dinner Vince brought was simple but delicious. There were overstuffed subway sandwiches, chips, pickles, water, and beer. As we ate, our conversation flowed easily. We talked about the gun range and all the fun I had.

Once we were full, we settled into a comfortable silence, the sky above us a canvas of twinkling stars. Vince handed me a beer, and I curled my legs beneath me, ready to soak in the tranquility of the moment. However, the quiet seemed to beckon deeper conversations, ones we hadn't ventured into before.

"This park has really come along nicely. It's actually really beautiful," Vince said, breaking the quiet.

I nodded. "Yeah. It's come a long way. The city really put a lot into it."

He took a swig of his beer as he looked around. "They really did. I've only been out here a couple of times. I'mma have to come more often. Maybe jog the trails."

I smirked at him over my beer. "Okay, I see you, Mr. Cartwright. Well, while you're jogging, I'll be having a coffee at Sips-N-Kicks over there." I pointed into the distance and in the general direction of my favorite coffee shop.

Vince chuckled. "You a mess, V, but I'll take you

up on that. I know you love your lil coffee shop and this park."

"Is that why you brought me here for dinner?" I asked.

He nodded, and I couldn't stop the smile that stretched across my face. This man was so thoughtful.

"Come here," I said as I leaned in. Vince met me halfway, and I kissed him softly on the lips. "You're something else. You know that?" I mumbled against his mouth.

"What you mean?" He asked.

"You pay attention. You're always checking on me and making sure I'm good. Like, you really listen, and I appreciate that. It's one of the things I adore about you," I told him.

Vince set his beer down and pulled me onto his lap so I could straddle him. The closeness and the feel of his dick twitching as I settled against him had my pussy leaking. 'Get it together, V. Stop being so nasty, girl,' I chastised myself.

Vince drew my focus back in when he said, "Of course I pay attention. Do you not know what you mean to me, Vanessa?" His dark eyes were serious as they bore into mine.

I did know how he felt about me. The man showed me on the regular, and I'm a firm believer in actions over words. And honestly, I loved how he loved on me. Vince was attentive, nurturing, and protective - everything a partner should be. And I wanted him in that way. I wanted him as a partner. But I also wanted Gage, and I just wasn't sure that Vince would be down with that.

I nibbled on my bottom lip and toyed with the beer bottle in my hand.

Vince tucked a finger under my chin and lifted my head, forcing me to meet his gaze. "You do know how I feel about you, right?"

I nodded. "I do...I just...I know you care about me, Vince. Hell, I know you more than care about me. You show me every time we're together."

"Okay...then what's up? I can tell something is bothering you." He ran a hand up and down my back, slowly coaxing me to open up.

"I don't know if I'm ready to talk about it yet, but there are things... things about me that you may not rock with and-"

He cut me off. "Sweetheart, I can't imagine anything about you that I wouldn't rock with. Trust me on that."

I wanted to tear my gaze from his, but he was still holding my chin hostage. "I don't know about that. Sometimes, when things get serious in a relationship, things change. Your partner expects different things. Expects you to change..."

"I hear you, and that's true in some cases. But, I'll tell you this. There is nothing, and I mean nothing, about you that I would change. You are everything, Vanessa Davis. You're smart, funny, wild, crazy as hell, fun as fuck," he released my chin and ran his thumb along my jawline. "And don't get me started on how beautiful and sexy you are."

I could have just melted right there in his damn lap. "Vince," I said, his name coming out in a choked whisper.

"I mean it, V. You're an incredible woman. And I know I don't really talk about my family, but listen, my mother, she was a lot like you."

My brow shot towards my hairline. It wasn't that Vince rarely talked about his family. It's that he never mentioned them at all. So to hear him say his mother was like me was surprising. "Really? She was?" I asked, intrigued.

"Yep," he replied.

"How so?" I was practically yelling in the man's face now. I hadn't meant to raise my voice; I was curious and excited to know what our similarities were.

"Well, for starters, she was loud," he said and bumped his nose against mine in jest.

I giggled. "My bad. I'm a little excited. You never talk about your family. Now quit playing and tell me more."

Vince wrapped his arms around my waist. He put one of his hands underneath my shirt and started drawing little circles against my skin. "My mom was... she was amazing."

"Was?" I questioned.

"Yeah. Her and my father passed a long time ago," he said.

I searched his face and could see the sadness just beneath the surface. "I'm sorry about your parents," I told him and kissed him softly on the chin.

"It's good. It's been a long time. My parents were great. My Dad was a really good man. He worked hard, played hard, and took care of us. But my mom though..." his eyes seemed to lose focus as if he was lost in some moment in the past. "She was amazing. And yes, she was loud, but she was kind and smart. And wild. Mom was a free spirit. Had me and my dad doing all kinds of crazy things. And I'm talking things that black folks don't really do." I laughed at that. "Like what?"

"Like when I was sixteen, she took me skydiving because she always wanted to try it."

My eyes bucked. "Skydiving? At sixteen? Is that even legal?"

Vince let out a low chuckle. "Not at all. You have to be eighteen. But Mom, she got around that requirement somehow, and to this day, I still go skydiving every once in a while."

"Wow. That's amazing. She sounds amazing - like she was a lot of fun," I told him.

"She was so much fun. And so free in her thoughts and her movements. She couldn't be tied down, and what I always admired about my father is that he never tried to." Vince brought his hands up and braced my face. His eyes bore into me, and I could feel my breathing pick up. "I see those same traits in you, Vanessa. You're such a breath of fresh air. You're fun, wild, and free - just like she was. It would be crazy of me to try and change that about you when it's what drew me to you in the first place. I want you just the way you are. Don't ever change. Not for me or anyone."

The comparison to his mother struck a chord deep within me, sending ripples through the waters of my heart. For a moment, I was caught off guard, the weight of his words settling around me like a warm blanket on a cold night. It was both an honor and a daunting realization, knowing I held a place in Vince's heart reminiscent of someone so pivotal.

His mother, clearly a beacon of light in his life, now reflected in his eyes when he looked at me. The gravity of that comparison wasn't lost on me —it was a bridge to a part of Vince's heart that I knew was sacred, a part he guarded fiercely. And here he was, not just letting me in but showing me that in me, he saw the same boundless spirit. To be seen in such light by Vince, to be loved for all that I am, just as fiercely as he had loved his mother, was an intimacy that touched me to the core. An intimacy that I hadn't known I craved.

But it also painted my current turmoil in even starker hues. Could someone who held me in such regard, who saw me as a mirror to the most important woman in his life, accept the divided state of my heart? The thought of revealing my love for Gage, of potentially fracturing this deepening connection with Vince, filled me with a dread so potent it was almost paralyzing.

Yet, as Vince's gaze held mine, a well of emotions swirling in those deep pools of chocolate, I felt a whisper of courage. Here was a man who wanted me for me, who saw in me a spirit akin to the one woman he clearly admired above all others. Maybe, just maybe, he could understand.

I hoped he could.

I needed him to.

As I stared into Vince's intense, sable gaze, I couldn't stop the tears that welled in my eyes. "Vince..." I started to tell him what his words meant to me, but he cut them off when he captured my mouth in the most toe-curling kiss.

It was as if he was trying to reach into the innermost parts of me. And he did. I felt him everywhere. In my veins, in my bloodstream, in the pit of my stomach, in my chest. I was completely undone.

The world around us melted away as Vince wrapped his tongue around mine, massaging it and making love to my mouth in that deep, slow, way he makes love to my pussy. Heat flooded my body, and I reached between us and rubbed my hands up his chest. Vince latched onto my tongue and sucked on it like it was his lifeline. My hips moved of their own volition, rocking against him. My panties soaked over as my arousal leaked from my pussy.

Vince pulled back from the kiss, and I groaned from the loss.

"Unh-Unh. Get back here," I growled and fisted his shirt and pulled him back to me. Before I could fuse my mouth back to his, my cell phone buzzed.

It was on the blanket next to me. I looked over at it to see that a text from Gage had come through. My already pounding heart took off in a sprint, and I shot Vince a quick glance.

"Answer. It's cool," he said and leaned back a bit, giving me some room to maneuver.

I stared at him for a minute. So many thoughts raced through my head. Did he see Gage's name? Is he upset? Is he telling me to respond to the text as a test?

As if reading my mind, Vince leaned in again and lightly brushed his finger across my lips before softly kissing them. "Respond to the text, Vanessa. It's good. I mean it," he said, then leaned back again.

I swallowed the nervous lump that had formed in my throat, grabbed my cell, and quickly responded to Gage's text. The pang of guilt at the interruption from Gage ate at me, while at the same time, my stomach fluttered as I read Gage's message.

Gage: I miss you, Dimples. I wish I could see you. Feel you. Taste you. You the only woman I've ever wanted to break training protocol for.

Me: Don't you dare, Emerson!

Gage: LOL! I'm not, but only because I know my girl doesn't date losers. And my opponent is a beast so I'mma stick to my training regimen and win this third belt for my baby girl.

Me: And better!

Gage: Oh, I am. But just know that after I win this fight, I'm taking you back to our suite and beating that pussy up!

My vagina literally thumped reading that last message. Gage had been sticking to his training program, and I hadn't seen him for the last two weeks. I missed his big, sexy, playful ass. I sent him one last message.

Me: She ready. We miss you, Daddy. Train hard. Can't wait for Vegas.

I set my phone back on the blanket and turned my attention back to Vince, who sat quietly, his gaze lifted to the stars. He didn't seem upset, and his energy hadn't shifted at all. I hoped Gage's text interruption hadn't fucked with mine because my nerves were tugging at my emotions.

Vince brought his gaze back to me, the soft glow from the moon casting shadows across his handsome face. His eyes were deep pools of chocolate. They held me captive as he leaned forward and pressed his forehead to mine. "I meant what I said, Vanessa. I love the woman you are. I rock with you. Ten toes down. There is nothing, and I mean nothing, I would change about you. All I want is for you to be happy. I mean that. Whatever happiness looks like to you, I'm with it."

This was it. This was the perfect moment for me to tell him about my feelings for Gage and what I wanted from both of them. But, I couldn't. I just couldn't. Vince's words, raw and sincere, were a balm to my tangled heart. They were also a reminder of the decision that lay ahead. I would eventually have to be honest with both men, and the thought of having that conversation high-key terrified me.

CHAPTER TWELVE

VINCE

The darkness of early morning wrapped around my home gym like a cocoon, pierced only by the soft glow of the lights I'd turned on, creating long shadows that stretched across the floor. I was in the middle of my workout; each rep set a way to push through the turmoil inside me. My body moved on autopilot, contrasting the storm of thoughts in my head.

With each transition from one exercise to the next, my mind couldn't help but wander to Vanessa and our date. Opening up to her about my mom and sharing those deeply personal memories was freeing and a little scary. My mother was my rock; her laughter and energy were a constant source of light in my life. I remembered her teaching me to appreciate the simple joys and to love wholeheartedly much like how I feel about Vanessa now.

I recalled Vanessa's laughter, the way her eyes lit up as I shared stories about my mom, giving me a sense of warmth that the cold weights in my hands couldn't match. But there was a thread of unease, too, pulled tight by the sight of Gage's name on her phone. She tried to hide it, but I saw the flicker of concern and uncertainty in her eyes.

Dropping the weights, the sound echoed in the gym, mirroring the clash within me. I knew Vanessa well. I knew she had feelings for Gage, even if she wouldn't admit it. I saw it at Griff and Gabby's engagement party and all over her face when she got that text. And though I hadn't confronted her about it, that unspoken truth had me a little nervous and wondering what it meant for us.

I leaned against the cool metal of the gym equipment, lost in thought. Could I share Vanessa with Gage? It was a heavy, complicated question. One I never thought I'd be considering. But sifting through my emotions, one thing stood out: my love for Vanessa was absolute. If her happiness meant including Gage in our lives, then maybe it was a path I needed to consider for her sake.

I saw my reflection across the room as dawn broke, filling the space with soft gold and amber light. There I was, at a crossroads, challenged to rethink what love meant to me. I always thought I knew, but now I wasn't so sure. Hell, the only thing I was sure of at this moment was that Vanessa was essential to my life. And if loving her meant embracing uncertainty or giving her her happiness in the full sense of the word, then I would do that for her.

I sighed deeply as I headed to my bedroom to shower and change. After taking care of my hygiene and getting dressed, I ate a quick breakfast and headed to the office. I got there earlier than normal this morning, hoping work would provide a distraction, but my relationship with Vanessa was still heavy on my mind as I checked my email and reviewed inquiries from potential clients.

Yara poked her head in my office door. "Hey, boss. You good for your meeting? You need me to sit in and take notes?" She asked.

"Nah. I'm good, Yara. Can you do me a favor, though?" I asked.

"Sure," she said, stepping inside my office. "What's up?"

"Can you order a bouquet of flowers for me? Something wild and exotic. And it must have jasmine in it."

Yara cocked her brow and eyed me up and down.

I lifted my hands in question. "What?"

A slow smile spread across Yara's face. "Nothing. I just... you're a really good guy, Boss."

"Thanks, Yara," I said as I slid a sticky note in her direction. "Have them delivered here."

"You got it," she said and grabbed the sticky note.

When I entered, Trace was already in the conference room. "What's up, Trace?" I greeted him.

"Sup," he said with a nod of his head.

Sigma came breezing in, a cup of coffee in his hand. "Sup, ya'll," he greeted us.

"Morning," I greeted back.

Trace just hit him with a head nod.

"Is the secure conference bridge open?" Sigma asked Trace, who nodded affirmatively. "Bet. Let's jump right in." He set his coffee down and leaned over the table, talking into the speakerphone. "What up, fam. E, you there?"

E's voice floated through the speakerphone. "I'm here, Boss."

"Alright. I want to start by thanking you and the team down there. The extraction of Dijana and the hit on that trafficking ring were textbook. Great job." Sigma looked over at me. You too, Vince. Great job on your first assignment. But I knew you would. Trace and I had zero doubts about bringing you on, and you proved us right."

"Thanks, man, I appreciate that," I said.

Sigma nodded, then returned his focus back to the speakerphone. "We've got a lot of job requests coming in. E, work with Vince on shifting through them and send me and Trace the ones you think we should take on."

"Got it," E said.

"Also, I meant what I said about taking down that trafficking ring. Trace and his intel team have uncovered some crucial information that will help us with that. I want to move on this quickly." He looked at Trace, who immediately started giving us the rundown on stash houses tied to the trafficking ring, outlining targets for our next operation.

"There are a lot of locations to hit, which means

we'll have a lot of teams out in the field. Vince, you'll be leading your own team on some of these raids. You good with that?"

"Absolutely," I told him.

"Bet. Next item: security for Gage's fight in Vegas. We'll follow the same protocol we normally do for him and his entourage. I'll be on point. E, you'll play second, and we'll need a few more guys due to the bigger entourage. Trace, send the list to E and put it on the big screen."

I watched as the large monitor on the wall lit up, and a list appeared on the screen. My eyes roamed over the names. Most I didn't know. My eyes slowed and lingered on the names I recognized. Gage, Griff, Gabby...Vanessa.

I felt my body stiffen at the sight of her name. Somehow, I knew her name would be there. It was one thing to speculate that she'd be going, but seeing her name on the list was a stark reminder of the complex web of emotions I found myself caught in. The thought of her with Gage, of sharing her, had always been a distant concern. Now, it felt all too real, pressing against my chest like a weight. It wasn't jealousy, though. My feelings for her were too clear and ran too deep for that, but a conversation needed to happen. I wasn't about to be disruptive before her trip, so I'd wait until after.

"It's only two additional people. I'll add Stryker and Hands to the detail," E said, her voice pulling me from my thoughts.

"Sounds good. Trace will be out of pocket while we're gone, so Vince, you'll hold down the fort here."

"I got you," I said.

"Alright, folks. That's all for now. Everybody good?"

A chorus of yeses, yeps, and yeahs floated through the speaker.

"Good. Let's get to work," Sigma said, then disconnected the line.

My phone buzzed as I was heading back to my office. Vanessa's name on the display had the corners of my mouth twitching. "What's up, beautiful?" I answered.

"Hey, good lookin'," she replied, and I could hear her smile through the phone. "I know you're working, so I'll be quick. Wanna go to an Escape Room with me, Gabby, and Griff tonight? Gabby's getting a little irritable with wedding planning, so I thought I'd take her and do something fun. Get her mind off the wedding for a little bit."

"Yeah, count me in, love." The decision to spend the evening with Vanessa, Gabby, and Griff was easy. It promised a respite from the internal debate raging within me about my future with Vanessa and how Gage fit into that picture. I knew Vanessa had deep feelings for me, and I knew where I stood —I'd fallen hard for her. I was in love with her, and I would continue to show her that regardless of the unconventional dynamics of our relationship.

"Yay," Vanessa squealed. I booked us a slot at

eight. Pick me up at seven-thirty."

"I got you.

"Okay. See you later, baby," Vanessa said, then hung up.

The emotional undercurrents of the morning's revelations lingered, and I slipped my professional mask in place as I sat at my desk. The world of tactical operations and security was one where I excelled, where things made sense. But navigating the complexities of my heart? That was proving to be the most challenging mission yet.

I spent the better part of the rest of the day on the line with E, going through potential clients. I really liked E. She was smart, tough, and deliberate in her assessments and feedback. As a former detective on the police force, I saw a lot of crime. I tackled a lot of crime but left so much out in the streets due to red tape. Something I didn't have to worry about working with Sigma and Trace. There was no red tape. We simply got things done, and because of that, we were able to help so many more people.

A little after five, I decided to call it quits for the day and head home to shower and change for my double date with Vanessa, Gabby, and Griff.

I pulled up to Vanessa's spot right at seven-thirty. She was heading out the door before I could get out and knock. I licked my lips as I watched her make her way to my truck. She was so damn gorgeous. The dark jeans she wore hugged her hips and thick thighs perfectly, and the cropped hoodie showed a sliver of her flat stomach. Her curls flowed wildly around her head, and those full lips of hers were a sweet berry color. Damn! My baby was fine.

I hopped out of the driver's seat to greet her. "Hey, love," I said, pulling her into my arms. "You look gorgeous as always," I said, then kissed her softly on the forehead.

Her smile was sweet as she looked up at me. "Thank you, baby. So do you. You ready for this lil double date?"

I shrugged. "Yeah, sure. Why?"

She leaned back in my arms and stared up at me. "Have you ever been to an Escape Room?"

"Nah."

"Well, I hope you're ready to be trapped in a series of rooms with me, Gabby, and Griff for the next two hours. The one I booked is supposed to be really challenging and take about two hours. I wanted to get Gabby focused on something else for a while. Wedding planning is getting to her."

"You're a good friend, V," I told her.

Her smile widened, and her eyes lit up. "That's what you took from everything I said?" She teased.

Instead of answering, I gave her a peck on the mouth, led her to the car's passenger side, opened the door, and helped her inside.

The drive to the Escape Room was pretty quick. Gabby and Griff were waiting outside when we arrived. The laughter and chatter of our group filled the air as we stepped into the dimly lit lobby of the escape room. The theme for tonight's challenge was "Heist at the Art Gallery," a setup that promised puzzles, teamwork, and a race against the clock to 'steal' a priceless painting. Vanessa squeezed my hand with excitement, her pretty eyes sparkling with anticipation.

"Thanks for setting this up, V.," Gabby said, smiling warmly at Vanessa.

"Anything for you, bestie. Besides, yo ass was getting a lil testy. This lil double-date was calculated," Vanessa laughed.

"Calculated or not, I'm glad you planned it. My woman can use this little break," Griff said, wrapping his arms around Gabby from behind and kissing her neck.

"Thank you, baby," Gabby told Griff, then narrowed her gaze on me and Vanessa. "Ya'll ready to show this escape room who's boss?" She asked.

"Oh, I've been ready," Vanessa beamed. We bout to take this escape room down."

"You do realize the goal here is to solve puzzles, not actually bring the place down, right?" Griff asked with a smirk.

Vanessa laughed, her gaze meeting mine. "Hear that, Vince? No breaking down doors and whatnot."

I chuckled, accepting the playful jab, then hit her with. "Sweetheart, I'm pretty sure Griff was talking about you when he said that."

Vanessa's head whipped in Griff's direction, and she burst out laughing at seeing the look on his face. He was absolutely talking about her.

"Whatever!" Vanessa playfully pouted. "Let's get this show on the road."

As we were led into the room by our game master, a young man with an enthusiastic demeanor, the reality of the challenge before us started to set in. The room was a marvel of creativity, designed to mimic an art gallery down to the smallest detail. Paintings hung on the walls, sculptures were placed at strategic points, and there were locked cases that I assumed held clues.

"Alright, folks. You have two hours to complete your heist. Remember, teamwork is key," the game master advised before locking us in the room.

Gabby immediately took charge, pointing out a large painting that seemed out of place. "That has to be our first clue," she declared, heading towards it.

Griff and I exchanged a look before following Vanessa and Gabby's lead. It was in these moments, solving puzzles and deciphering codes, that I saw another side to Vanessa. The lawyer in her was front and center, with her sharp mind and keen observation skills on full display. But it was her infectious laughter whenever we found a clue or solved a puzzle that pulled at my heartstrings.

At one point, while Vanessa and Gabby were examining a sculpture for hidden compartments, Griff and I found ourselves working on a digital keypad lock.

"You and Vanessa seem to really get along," Griff

remarked casually, his eyes not leaving the keypad as we punched in numbers.

"Yeah, you know, V. She's good people. We click, you know? She's... she's amazing," I admitted, feeling a warmth spread through me.

Griff nodded, a knowing smile on his face. "Yeah, she good people for sure. A bit loud and wild at times but so genuine and giving. That woman will do anything for Gabby, and I love her for that. She is who she is, and you can't help but rock with that."

"True that," I agreed as I was reminded of the complicated web that was my love life with Vanessa. I wondered if Griff knew about her and Gage. Hell, of course, he did. He and Gage went way back. They were boys. It made me wonder more what he thought about it all. Both of us dating the same woman. I was tempted to ask him but decided against it because, deep down, the only person's viewpoint that mattered to me was Vanessa's. So instead, I focused on solving these puzzles.

After several more puzzles, unlocking two additional rooms, lots of laughter, and a few moments of intense concentration, we heard the sound we had been waiting for—the lock of the door clicking open, signaling our success.

"We did it!" Vanessa exclaimed, high-fiving Gabby and then rushing over to me. "We didn't even have to break anything," she joked.

Her excitement was contagious, and she was so

damn cute. I couldn't help but scoop her up in a bear hug and bury my face in her neck. "Yes, we did good. You did good, Love," I mumbled against the fragrant skin of her neck.

"Alright, you two, break it up. We can't be getting kicked out of this place because you two are some horny asses," Gabby joked.

"Umm, don't do us," Vanessa clapped back but pulled me towards the exit.

"This was fun," Gabby commented as we stepped outside.

Vanessa beamed. "I'm glad you had a good time."

"I did. And Vince, thanks for coming out and putting up with me and Vanessa's shenanigans. Poor Griff has to deal with us all the time. I know he appreciated having you as a buffer."

I chuckled. "It's good. I enjoyed myself. Happy to tag along anytime."

"I'mma remember that," Griff threatened, and we all laughed.

The ladies hugged goodbye while Griff and I dapped each other up. A few minutes later, we were back in my truck, heading to Vanessa's place.

We rode in silence, letting the old-school sounds of Mint Condition engulf us. As I drove, I thought about the puzzles in the Escape Room and how they were like the challenges I was facing in this relationship - complex, sometimes frustrating, but ultimately solvable if we communicate and work together.

I rolled the window down, the night air was cool

and crisp as Vanessa and I made our way back to her place, our laughter, and conversation trailing behind us like the tail of a comet. The double date with Gabby and Griff had been a good time—a perfect blend of challenge and fun that had us all working together and strengthening bonds.

Vanessa let out a soft yawn as we entered her home.

"Tired?" I asked and rubbed my hand softly across her lower back.

"Yeah, a bit," Vanessa admitted with another yawn. "But in the best way. Tonight was so much fun."

"It was," I agreed and guided her towards the bathroom. How about we take a shower, get cleaned up, and relax?"

Vanessa smiled, her eyes lighting up at the suggestion. "That sounds perfect."

I turned on the shower and then helped Vanessa undress. My eyes roamed over her naked flesh with each article of clothing I removed. I kissed her softly on the lips before helping her into the shower.

"Join me," she crooned with a sly smile and sexed over eyes.

I quickly shed my clothes and joined her.

The shower was hot and inviting. Water cascaded over us in soothing rivulets.

"Let me clean you up," Vanessa said as she grabbed a washcloth and squirted some of her jasmine-scented body wash onto it.

The muscles in my stomach flexed as she moved behind me and ran the washcloth over my shoulders, down my back and buttocks, and down to my ankles. The way she slowly ran the washcloth over my body and the silkiness of the soap had my man's thickening. Vanessa noticed as she made her way around to the front of me. Her eyes deepened with lust as she bit down into her bottom lip and let out a small moan as she stared down at my now fully hard and throbbing dick.

"Did I do that?" She teased, reaching for my man.

I grabbed her wrist, halting her movement before she could grab it. "Hell yeah, you did that." I pulled her against me, our wet bodies slippery against each other. I moved the wrist I was holding behind her back and held it there. I wrapped my other hand around her throat and used my body to move her backward until she was pressed between me and the shower wall.

I stared down at her, pinning her with my eyes. "You know what your touch does to me, love," I whispered against her mouth.

Her breathing was labored, her chest rising and falling rapidly. With each movement, her turgid nipples brushed against my chest. "And you know what yours does to me," she breathed out.

I grinned and slipped my thigh between hers and rubbed it against her clit, soaked from the shower and her arousal. "This pussy so wet for me," I told her, then swiped my tongue across her mouth.

"Vince," she moaned and rubbed her pussy against my thigh.

"What do you need, love? Tell me?"

"I need you to..."

"You need me to what?" I asked as I nibbled on her lips and jawline.

"I need you to fuck me," she whined and bucked her hips.

She was so worked up. I loved that shit, but she would have to wait a minute. I needed my fill of her. I captured her mouth, kissing and nibbling on her plump lips before driving my tongue inside and claiming every part of her mouth. She moaned, and I pulled back, pressing soft kisses along her throat and shoulders.

"Vince," she called my name on a needy plea.

There was an intense desire in me to have her so needy that she was practically climbing the walls for me. So, I ignored her pleas and took her mouth again, deepthroating her with my tongue and swallowing up her pleas. I slightly tightened the grip I had on her throat as I brought my other hand to her sex and ran two fingers up her soaked slit.

Vanessa hissed and circled her hips against my hand. "God, yes," she moaned into my mouth.

I shoved those same two fingers inside her, fucking her fast, hard, and deep while kissing her with the same fervor.

Vanessa bucked and gyrated, working her hips against my hand. I could feel her walls pulsing and tightening around my fingers.

"Yes! Yes! God, yes!" Vanessa cried.

She was so close to the edge, but I wasn't ready for her to come yet. I slipped my fingers out of her, and she groaned.

"No, no, no. Don't stop. Please. I'm so close," she whined.

I grinned down at her. "Oh, I know. Your little hot box had a death grip on my fingers," I teased.

She poked her lips out in the cutest pout. "Stop playing and make me come. Please, Vince. I need it. I need you."

Shit! That did it. I wanted her needy for me, and she was, but now, with those three little words, I was just as needy. I needed to be buried deep inside her. I needed to feel her warm walls pulling me in and drowning me in her essence.

I barely recognized the roar that erupted from me as I gripped her thighs and lifted her up. She quickly wrapped her legs around me. I cupped her ass, spreading her cheeks, and entered her in one full, hard, deep thrust. Her cry of pleasure filled the steamy space as I drilled into her. Very quickly, I could feel her walls spasm and tighten.

"You about to come?" I whispered against her throat.

"Yes, yes. Yes. I'm about to...to come," she stuttered as her walls clamped down on me.

I reached down and pressed my thumb against her clit, and Vanessa's entire body seized up as she let out a guttural moan.

"Come for me, love," I coaxed.

That did it. Vanessa came hard, her screams of pleasure filling the bathroom.

I gripped her ass, spreading her cheeks wide, and slammed into her, fucking her through her orgasm. I loved how tight she felt around me and the love faces she made. She was so fucking beautiful when she came. It was more than enough to have me exploding inside her. My orgasm was swift and violent as I pumped my seed deep into her womb.

Making love in the shower, with the steam and the heat enveloping us, was an experience that transcended the physical. It was as if the water was washing away any barriers between us, leaving us bare in every sense of the word.

After, as we dried off, I reached for the bottle of jasmine oil on Vanessa's vanity.

"Lay down," I told her as I nodded my head towards the bed.

She cocked her head and narrowed her eyes on me. "So, you going full-service tonight?" She smirked.

"Don't I always?" I countered.

"You do. But tonight, you coming with extras. Me likey," she said as she moved towards the bed.

I licked my lips as I watched her sprawl out on the bed on her stomach, her round ass poked in the air. I climbed onto the bed and straddled her thighs, careful not to put my full weight on her. I warmed the oil between my hands before beginning to massage her muscles, the tactile sensation of her skin beneath my fingers both soothing and electrifying.

The soft glow of the lamp on the nightstand danced across the room, casting a warm, intimate light. The scent of the jasmine oil filled the air, a heady mix that seemed to deepen our connection. As I worked the oil into her shoulders, her back, and her legs, I could feel her relaxing and melting under my touch.

It was in this quiet, vulnerable space that our conversation drifted to the future. I talked about my work with Sigma and Trace, about the good we aimed to do by taking down those who preyed on the innocent.

Vanessa shared her dreams for her law career, her passion for justice and change shining through. She spoke fondly of Gabby and her upcoming wedding, how obsessed she was with Gabby and Griff's relationship, and how perfect they were for each other. She talked about everything. Well, everything except for her own relationships. I could sense the hesitation to go there, and again, I chose not to press, not out of fear, but out of respect. I wanted her to come to me, in her own time, with her whole heart.

CHAPTER THIRTEEN

GAGE

The gym was quiet now; the final echoes of my second training session of the day faded into a heavy stillness. I leaned against the ropes of the ring, chest heaving, sweat dripping down my brow and onto the canvas floor. The smell of hard work and determination hung thick in the air, a testament to the hours of preparation I'd put in for this upcoming fight. The only noises that broke the silence were the sound of my breathing and the occasional thud of my gloves against the bag. The anticipation of the fight was a constant hum in my veins, a mix of adrenaline and an almost tangible eagerness to step into the ring.

Griff's voice sliced through the silence, grounding me back in reality. "Yo, you good?" His figure was silhouetted against the dim lighting of the gym, an ever-present pillar in the chaos of my professional life.

Dropping my guard, I let out a breath, the tension momentarily lifting. "Yeah, just thinking about Vegas," I admitted, peeling off my gloves. The leather felt heavy in my hands, weighted with expectation.

Griff climbed into the ring and stood a few feet away from me. "What's up? I know you not worried about the fight. You're more than ready," he assured, clapping me on the shoulder. His confidence was infectious, but it was Vanessa that dominated my thoughts. I was ready to get this fight over with so I could have my way with her all over my hotel suite. This celibate shit, with her in my life, was whack as fuck.

"Nah. I ain't never been worried about a fight. I'm more than ready," I assured him.

Griff's brow lifted as he stared at me. "Then what's up? Something's clearly on your mind, bruh."

I shrugged and sucked my teeth. "Nah. It's good. Just some typical man shit. You know how it is. I'm just ready for this fight to be over so I can get some ass, my nigga," I laughed.

Griff chuckled. "So, you not worried about the fight. Yo' ass is concerned with getting pussy after the fight."

My laughter mingled with Griff's, echoing through the gym. "Hell yeah! I ain't had no pussy in a minute."

"I'm sure it hasn't been that long, Gage," Griff scoffed.

"Tell that to my dick, nigga," I clapped back.

Griff shook his head. "Well, shit, there are plenty of women in Vegas. Take your pick. Showgirl. Escort-"

I cut him off. "Aw, hell nah. Won't be no

showgirls, escorts, or regular hoes. I'm talking about Vanessa. You know she coming to the fight, right?"

"Oh yeah, that's right. I did know that. So, how are things going with y'all?" He asked, a knowing smirk playing on his lips.

His question hung in the air, heavy with unsaid implications. I knew he knew that Vanessa was seeing both me and Vince, and I also knew that he would never outright bring that shit up, but he'd talk through it with me if I did. "Things are good. Great actually. Vanessa is...well shit, for me, she's about as close to perfection as any woman can get."

"Damn," was all Griff said.

"Yeah," I agreed, knowing full well what that 'damn' meant. "She's got a hold on me, man. Can't even lie about it. Never felt this way about anyone before. She's mine, and I don't plan on letting her go ever... if that's what she wants."

"Have y'all talked about your relationship? Where it's going?" He asked.

I shook my head. "Not so much. Not like that anyway. I mean, we're a live-in-the-moment type couple. You know?"

"I get that, but don't you want to really know where y'all stand?" Griff pressed.

I knew where Griff was leading me to in this conversation. For everything I had said up to now, I never mentioned exclusivity, and that fact lingered in the space between us.

Griff's gaze was piercing - knowing when he

said, "Okay. So, what you're saying is that you're all in with Vanessa. No matter what."

Griff's gaze never wavered as he waited for my response. The weight of his question hung in the air like a heavy bag I was about to punch the hell out of, but instead, it hit me square in the chest. His eyes held that same intensity they did when he was in the ring, but this time, it wasn't about fighting; it was about Vanessa and where I stood in all of this.

"Let me ask you like this, so you cool with sharing Vanessa with Vince?" His voice was calm, like he was asking something as simple as the time of day. But I knew Griff, and I knew he didn't ask simple questions.

I let out a long breath, the kind that comes from the gut, the kind you take when you're about to say something that's been clawing at the back of your mind for a while. "It ain't about being cool with it, Griff," I began, picking my words like I was walking on glass. "It's about understanding what she needs, what she wants, what makes her happy." I paused, letting that settle in the space between us. "And I know you know what I'm talking about."

He nodded, then asked. "Do you love her?"

Yes, was the immediate response in my head. But shit, that's because it's been true for a minute now. But admitting it out loud, even to my boy, Griff? That was something else.

"Vanessa is... the best thing I never knew I needed. You know me, Griff. I didn't want for nothing - I thought I had it all... until her. She showed me what was missing. That woman is... my perfect match. Wild, free, full of sass, and untamable. Why would anyone want to change something that beautiful? So, when you ask me if I love her... yeah, I do. And if sharing her with Vince makes her happy, then yeah, I'd do it. If that's what she wants."

Griff raised an eyebrow, waiting for me to continue. I could tell he was measuring my words, seeing if they matched the truth in my eyes.

"I'm serious, man. When it comes to Vanessa, it's like... I don't wanna change her in any way. I fell for her because of who she is - that wild spirit, that fire. It's what makes her, her. And if Vince is a part of that happiness, then I gotta be good with it. Ain't no point in trying to clip a butterfly's wings."

Griff leaned back against the ropes, nodding slowly. "So, you're saying you're good as long as she's happy. Even if that happiness includes another man."

"Yeah," I said, surer of my words now. "Exactly that. I ain't never been the jealous type. It's just not in me. And honestly, it ain't like me and Vince hate each other or anything. We respect each other, and we both care about Vanessa. I just wanna see her smile, see her live the life she wants. I'm happy when she's happy."

Griff studied me for a minute, and then a slow smile spread across his face. "You really are caught up, huh?"

I chuckled, shaking my head. "You don't even know the half of it. I'm all the way fucked up behind this girl, man. And I'm okay with that. Vanessa, she's special. I don't wanna lose that because I'm too busy tryna fit her into some box she don't belong in."

"That's real," Griff said, his voice full of respect. "You're a good dude, Gage. I respect how you handling this. Most men would bounce or try to make her choose."

I chuckled. "I really ain't doing either right now, if I'm honest. We don't talk about it. Like, I know she's seeing him but... it's like whatever she got with him is so far removed from what we got that it don't even register when we together. Not to diminish what she has with him; it just doesn't impact what I have with her. You know?"

Griff shook his head. "No. I don't know. I could never share Gabby. I'm too fucking possessive behind that woman. But like I said, you're a good man, Gage. And shit, love looks different for everybody. I support that shit, whatever it is," Griff added as he held out his hand. We dapped each other up, and Griff pulled me in for a brief hug, slapping me on the back. "Phew, shit. Let's hit the showers." he chuckled. "We smell like the wrong end of a boxing glove."

I laughed and followed him out of the wring. Griff headed to the private bathroom in his office, and I headed to the private showers in the locker room. The sound of the water hitting the tiles as I showered was the only noise in the room, but my mind was still on Vanessa. I was standing there, letting the hot water run over me, washing away the sweat and tension from the day's training, but my thoughts were miles away: in the future, in Vegas, in a hotel suite with Vanessa. I could see it so clearly—the way she'd look at me, that mischievous grin on her face, and the way her thick ass body would feel wrapped around mine after all this time apart.

By the time I got out of the shower and dressed, my resolve was set. I wasn't gonna waste time wondering about what might happen. I knew what I wanted, and in Vegas, I was gonna make sure Vanessa knew that too.

The drive home was quiet, just the sound of my engine humming and my loud ass thoughts. My mind was still tangled up in thoughts of Vanessa and what our future might look like. When I finally pulled up to my spot, I grabbed my phone and dialed her number. I needed to hear her voice. The phone barely rang before her sweet voice came through the line, light, and teasing, like she knew I was missing her.

"Hey, handsome. Miss me already?" She greeted, her voice flirty and teasing.

I chuckled, leaning back into the leather seats of my car. "You already know. Yo lil ass is in my system. "

"I better be," she shot back, but there was warmth in her tone that made my chest tighten.

"Fa sho, love," I said. "But look, I just finished training and was thinking about Vegas. I can't wait to get your sexy ass out there - to have you on my arm after I win that fight. You know I'mma fuck you all over that penthouse suite when it's all said and done, right?"

Vanessa giggled. "You better. I'm excited for the trip. Gabby and I are going shopping tomorrow to grab a few things."

"Oh, word?"

"Yeah. I need to get something to match your colors for the fight. That way, there'll be no doubt who I'm rooting for," she replied.

"I feel that. And I kind of like the idea of you wearing my colors. Emerald green's gonna look so good on you, baby girl," I complimented.

I could hear the smile in her voice when she said, "I know, right? We're gonna have so much fun, Gage. I just know it's gonna be a wild ass time."

"It will definitely be that," I said, my voice dropping a little, teasing her the way I knew she liked."

She laughed, that low, sexy sound that drove me wild. "Don't be using your sex voice on me when you know you have to remain celibate until after the fight."

I grinned. "You mean this voice?" I said, using the same tone.

"Yeah, that one. It's already got my kitty leaking," she said.

"Shit! Send me a lil pic of my favorite girl," I told her.

She giggled. "Oh, she's your favorite girl?"

"She's attached to you, so yeah," I replied.

"Cute. But, nope. I'm not gonna be the reason you lose the fight," she said.

I frowned. "What you mean?"

"You're supposed to be abstinent until after the fight. I don't want my pum-pum to be the reason you lose the fight."

I laughed. "Girl, you trippin'-"

"Nope. Unh-unh. Not doing it. In fact, let me get off this phone with you before I get tempted. You know what you do to me, Gage Emerson. So, I'm gonna bid you a good day. Besides, I have a meeting in five minutes."

"Whatever, tease," I joked. "I'll hit you up later."

"Bye, handsome," Vanessa said, then hung up.

I shook my head as I tossed my phone onto the passenger seat. A minute later, it buzzed. I snatched it up and saw a message from Vanessa. I opened it, and my dick immediately stiffened. She'd sent a picture. I stared at it, my jaw tightening, a slow grin spreading across my face. Damn, she knew how to push my buttons. Her shirt unbuttoned just enough to give me a glimpse of that lacy black bra, the curve of her cleavage daring me to forget every damn thing and think only of her. My dick was already straining against my pants, but it wasn't just about getting off. Vanessa had me hooked—mind, body, and soul.

And she knew it.

Vegas was gonna be something else.

CHAPTER FOURTEEN

VANESSA

The smell of fresh espresso and baked goods filled the air as I pushed open the door to Sips-N-Kicks, the familiar chime of the bell above the entrance announcing my arrival. I spotted Gabby at our usual table by the window, her head buried in a wedding planner, surrounded by a mess of color-coded tabs and sticky notes. I couldn't help but smile. We were down to the last bit of planning for her upcoming nuptials, and I couldn't be more excited that my bestie's wedding day was fast approaching.

I slid into the seat across from her, setting my oversized bag on the seat beside me.

"Morning, bridezilla," I teased, reaching for the cup of coffee waiting for me. Gabby had already ordered my favorite macchiato with an extra shot of espresso. She knew me too well.

Gabby glanced up, rolling her eyes but smiling anyway. "I see you got jokes this morning."

I laughed. "And do. But that's because you over here looking all serious and focused."

Gabby shook her head. "My wedding's in like four months, V. Not only am I serious, but I'm stressed."

I reached over and placed a hand over hers. "Well, don't worry. Your girl is here. I got you. You know that."

She nodded and leaned back in her chair, her smile softening as she looked at me. "I know, and thank you. I can't believe it's almost here. Where has the time gone?"

"You know what they say? Time flies when you're having fun, and you and Griff been having a whole lot of fun since ya'll got together," I told her with a wink.

"You right," Gabby said. "I just hope the wedding and reception is as fun."

"It will be," I assured her. "Everything's going to be perfect."

We spent the next half hour going over the last few details, talking through seating arrangements, playlists, and final RSVPs. The easy rhythm of our conversation, the back-and-forth banter, was comforting, a reminder of the simple things that anchored us through life's changes.

As we wrapped up the wedding talk, Gabby leaned back in her chair, a mischievous grin creeping onto her face. "So... Vegas."

I felt my own excitement stir at the mention. "Oh, it's about to be wild. You know that, right?"

Gabby's eyes sparkled. "I know. Trust. We get to see our first live fight from a behind-the-curtain viewpoint. Griff told me we get all access being a part of Gage's entourage, and they've planned out the entire weekend. Fancy dinners, private gambling rooms, VIP club access. This is gonna be one hell of a weekend."

"Damn right. I already know we're gonna turn all the way up. I'm thinking about getting something real sexy for the fight, too—something that matches Gage's colors."

Gabby nodded approvingly. "Yes, you have to. Emerald green, right? That color on you? That man is not gonna know what hit him. You're going to look so damn fine, V."

I laughed, feeling a little of the tension I'd been carrying around ease away. But then Gabby's next words pulled me back into the unease I was trying to escape.

"And safety won't be a problem. We're going to be well taken care of. Griff has Sigma and Trace handling security for Gage out in Vegas," Gabby said casually, her attention more focused on the next sip of her coffee than the bomb she'd just dropped.

My heart skipped a beat, and I forced a casual nod. "Oh, for real? That's what's up," I said, trying to keep my tone light.

Gabby looked up; her eyes sharp. "Yeah. Don't worry, though. Vince isn't going. He's staying behind to hold down the fort."

"How do you know?" I asked.

"Griff told me."

The relief that washed over me was almost dizzying. "Good to know," I managed, taking a longer sip of my coffee to cover my reaction.

Gabby leaned in, her voice softening. "Don't worry, V. We're gonna have a good time. You get to leave your relationship struggles right here in Eastbrook and have a little carefree fun in Vegas."

I nodded. "You're right. I'm going to leave all my relationship drama, the nerves, and the tension here in Eastbrook and have a blast in Vegas."

She studied me for a moment longer before nodding. "Alright, that's my girl. That's what I wanna hear. And you know I got your back no matter what, right?"

"Always," I said, giving her a reassuring smile. "Now, let's go get you fitted in that dress, and then it's shopping time. We gotta make sure we're the two baddest bitches in Vegas next weekend."

Gabby's laughter rang out, easing the tension that had crept into the conversation. As we gathered our things and headed out of Sips-N-Kicks, I had a newfound excitement for the Vegas trip.

The chime above the door jingled as Gabby and I walked into the bridal shop, the kind of place that practically smelled like happily-ever-after. The showroom was all white and gold, a sea of lace and satin gowns that shimmered under the soft lighting. Gabby was buzzing with excitement as we approached the fitting area. This was her moment, and I was glad to be here, soaking in her joy.

"Alright, bestie, let's see this dress one more

time," I said, giving her a playful nudge as we reached the fitting room. Gabby grinned and disappeared behind the curtain.

A few minutes later, she emerged, the dress clinging to her curves in all the right places. It was perfect—an elegant blend of modern and classic, with a sweetheart neckline that made her glow.

"Damn, Gabs. Griff ain't gon' know what hit him when he sees you in that," I said, my voice filled with genuine awe.

Gabby twirled in front of the mirror, her smile wide and carefree. "I hope so. I just want everything to be perfect."

"It will be," I assured her. "You killin' the wedding game in that dress, girl. It was made for you."

We spent the next few minutes adjusting the train and tweaking the fit here and there, the bridal consultant fluttering around, pinning and adjusting until Gabby was satisfied. Once she was out of the dress and back in her regular clothes, the mood shifted from bridal bliss to full-on Vegas excitement.

"Alright, let's hit up these boutiques," Gabby declared as we left the shop. "Griff gave me his black card. Said our little shopping spree for Vegas was on him."

The grin that spread across my face was huge. "Say less, bestie," I told her. "See, that's why we love Griff. He knows how to keep us happy," I added.

Gabby laughed, loud and full-throated. "He do

though," she agreed as we headed out the door.

We spent the next couple of hours hopping from one boutique to another, trying on dress after dress, shoe after shoe. Gabby was all about the sparkle—sequins, rhinestones, anything that would catch the light on the Vegas strip. I, on the other hand, had my eyes set on something bold, something that would make Gage's jaw drop the second he saw me.

I ended up with an emerald green dress, slinky and fitted, the kind that hugged every curve like it was custom-made for me. It was perfect—a nod to Gage's fight colors, and sexy as hell.

"Oh, that's the one right there," Gabby said, eyeing me up and down as I stepped out of the fitting room. "Gage is gonna lose his damn mind when he sees you in that."

I struck a playful pose, my hips swaying as I admired myself in the mirror. "That's the plan, sis."

As we paid for our purchases, the conversation drifted back to Vegas. Gabby was practically bouncing with excitement, her energy infectious.

"I can't wait to get out there," she said, taking her shopping bag from the cashier. "It's gonna be my last big hoorah as a single woman. Well, not single, but you know what I mean."

"I do, and you know what this means, don't you?" I asked, and Gabby looked at me expectantly. "It means that we need to end your single life with a bang. We're gonna dance. We're gonna pop bottle and be the baddest bitches in Vegas next weekend."

"And let's not forget that we'll be on the arms of two of the finest black men on the planet," Gabby added.

"I know that's right," I said high-fiving her.

Gabby's laughter rang out as we headed out of the last boutique, the sun setting behind us. It had been a long, fun-filled day with my bestie. As we walked to my car, bags in hand, I felt the excitement start to build again, even if there was a tiny sliver of anxiety lurking in the background. Vegas was just around the corner, and I was determined to make the most of it.

***

The late afternoon sun cast a golden hue over the Eastbrook airport as we made our way toward the private jet that would whisk us away to Vegas. Airline personnel were already loading the last of the luggage onto the plane as we arrived, and I couldn't help but admire the sleek, luxurious jet waiting on the tarmac. This was the kind of high life I'd only ever seen in movies, and now, here I was, about to experience it firsthand.

The second I stepped onto the jet, the sheer luxury of it hit me like a wave. Plush leather seats in a rich cream color lined the cabin, while polished mahogany tables gleamed under the ambient lighting. A stewardess greeted us with a warm smile, offering a tray of champagne flutes filled with bubbles that sparkled just as brightly as the Vegas lights I imagined in my head.

I settled into a seat next to Gabby, directly

across from Gage and Griff, who had already made themselves comfortable. Gabby nudged me with her elbow, her eyes sparkling with excitement as she took in the scene. "Girl, we really out here living," she whispered, her tone dripping with glee. "This is how the other half lives, I guess."

I chuckled and took a sip of my champagne, the crisp bubbles dancing on my tongue. "Yeah, it's a whole other level. Get used to it, Mrs. Soon-to-be Thayer, because your man, your man, your man, is a muthafuckin' baller."

Gabby giggled, the sound filled with joy. "Our men are ballers. Our men," she said with extra emphasis on the word 'Our'.

As the jet began to taxi down the runway, I felt a buzz of excitement course through me. This weekend wasn't about my complicated love life. This weekend was about fun, pure and simple. And I planned on making the most of it.

The stewardess came by to collect our empty glasses, and I settled into my seat, the soft leather molding to my body as I let out a contented sigh. I glanced over at Gage, who was watching me with that familiar, heated gaze, the kind that always sent a thrill down my spine. I flashed him a playful smile as I reached into my bag and pulled out a deck of cards. "You ready to lose, handsome?" I teased, holding up the cards.

"Lose? Oh, sweetheart, you know your man better than that. I don't lose. I told you that," Gage smirked.

"We'll see about that. Me and Gabbs against you and Griff," I said, getting up. "Switch seats with me so I'm across from my partner."

Gage grinned at me as he got up and switched seats with me. Very quickly, the cabin filled with the sounds of shuffling cards, playful banter, and laughter. I could feel the tension in my shoulders easing as the game progressed, my focus shifting to the cards in my hand and the competitive spirit that always seemed to emerge when we played.

Gabby and I worked in sync, just like old times, talking shit and laughing loud as we racked up the books. Gage and Griff tried their best to catch up, but it was clear from the jump that they were no match for us.

"That's game right there," Gabby shouted as she slammed her final card down on the table, sealing our victory.

I threw my head back in laughter, feeling lighter than I had in days. "Guess you were ready to lose, handsome. Guess we all can't be winners. I mean, we are," I gloated, giving Gabby a high five.

Gage grumbled under his breath, shaking his head as he gathered the cards. "Y'all got lucky this time. Ain't no way you running that back."

I leaned forward, resting my elbows on the table as I met his gaze. "Oh, you big mad, huh? Can't handle losing to two beautiful women?"

Gage's eyes narrowed, but there was a playful glint in them that sent a shiver down my spine. "Even when I lose, I win, baby girl. You'll see soon enough."

I raised an eyebrow, feeling my heart pick up speed as he held my gaze a moment longer than necessary. I knew that look all too well—the one that said he was about to get me into trouble, the kind of trouble I loved but knew I shouldn't give in to. Not here. Not now. But damn, did I want to.

We cleared the table, the banter continuing as the stewardess came by with another round of drinks. I was still riding the high of our win when I felt Gage's hand on my lower back as I stood up to stretch. His touch was light, but it sent a jolt of heat through my body, one that settled low in my belly.

"I'm going to run to the bathroom," I murmured, trying to play it cool as I stepped away.

Gage was hot on my heels as I looked over my shoulder. I didn't stop; I kept moving to the back of the plane, where the bathrooms were located. There were two of them. I opened the door and slipped into one. I tried to quickly close the door, but Gage stuck the tip of his shoe in the way, so I couldn't close it.

I shot him a warning look, but he just grinned, all innocent, though his eyes were anything but. "Gage..."

"Nah," he said, gently pushing me back into the bathroom. "I told you, gorgeous, even when I lose, I win," he continued as he closed the door and locked it.

I backed up, looking around as I did.

The bathroom was bigger than the bathrooms normally on planes, and it was luxurious. It was actually full-sized, sleek, and modern, with marble countertops and a full shower. Impressive.

I stopped moving when my backside hit the sink. I stared at Gage, who looked at me like I was his next meal. "Hey. I-I don't know what you think you're doing, Mister, but you know you can't be getting jiggy until after the fight," I stammered.

Gage's grin widened, but he didn't say anything. He closed the distance between us in one stride and pulled me close, his mouth finding mine in a heated kiss.

"Gage, baby, we can't," I mumbled against his lips, though I made no move to push him away.

"Just a lil taste, sweetheart," he rasped against my earlobe before taking it between his teeth and gently biting down.

I gasped and arched into him as Gage's hand slipped under my dress and slowly slid up my thigh. His fingers danced along the edge of my panties before slipping beneath the fabric. The heat from his touch radiated through me like wildfire; all thoughts of denial vanished.

Tugging down my panties with a single swift motion, Gage lowered himself onto his knees before me. The cool air hit my exposed flesh as Gage drew lines with his tongue from my inner thigh to the apex of my desire.

"Gage, we can't..." I tried to protest but was silenced by the skillful movements of his tongue—

sliding, probing, teasing. He knew exactly what to do to drive me wild, and I gripped the countertop, the skin on my knuckles pulling tight as I tried not to cry out.

His mouth found its way back to my clit, sucking and flicking it with an expertise that sent shudders through my frame. I felt a heat building within me, a pressure that begged for release.

"G-Gage... please. Baby.... I-I-I... I'm..." My words died in my throat as my orgasm hit.

"Mmm... that's right. Come for daddy, love. Come for me," Gage mumbled against my pussy as he continued his assault.

As my pleasure crescendoed, my legs turned to jelly beneath me. I closed my eyes against the onslaught of pleasure while Gage lapped up every drop that spilled from my center.

"Mmm... so good, V. So fucking good," he murmured as he licked me clean.

My thighs were still quaking when Gage rose to his feet, his lips wet from our intimate exchange. His pupils were blown with lust as he stared down at me.

"You don't know how bad I wanna splinter that tight little pussy right now. I swear this fight can't come fast enough," he growled, then dipped his head and kissed me, his tongue invading my mouth, laden with the salty-sweet taste of my own release.

I whimpered as he deepened the kiss, his hands wandering over the soft contours of my body. Our lips moved together, tongues tangling in a dance as intoxicating as the sexual high we'd just shared.

Finally, pulling back with a sigh, Gage caressed my cheek with his knuckles. The look in his eyes was intense, reverent, satisfied... possessive. He wet a cloth from the sink and began to gently clean me up, his touch soothing on my sensitive skin.

I watched as he kneeled back down, plucked my wet panties from around my ankle, and tucked them into his pocket with a smirk. The audacity of it caused a surprised laugh to bubble up from my chest.

"Can I have my panties, please, Sir?" I asked with a grin.

He shook his head. "Nah. I'll be keeping these," he proclaimed, patting the pocket he'd stored them in.

"Gage," I pouted and reached for him, but he was too fast. Before I could grip his shirt, he was already opening the bathroom door and exiting. "Ass," I whisper-yelled after him, but he just chuckled and kept moving to his seat.

I closed the bathroom door and faced the mirror. I definitely looked like a woman who was very recently satisfied—and I felt it too, a warmth spreading through me, reminding me of how Gage always knew exactly how to get under my skin in the best way. My dress was a little askew, my skin was flushed, and my pupils were still slightly blown from my orgasm. I closed my eyes and inhaled deeply to gather myself. Once I felt like I was semi-together, I headed back to my seat.

Gabby gave me a knowing look, but she didn't say anything; she just raised an eyebrow and smirked. I rolled my eyes at her, but inside, my heart was racing, both from what had just happened and from the knowledge that Vegas was only a few hours away.

CHAPTER FIFTEEN

VANESSA

The dry desert heat hit me as soon as we stepped off the jet; the sun was already dipping low in the sky and casting long shadows across the tarmac. There was a nervous flutter in my stomach as I followed behind Gage, his hand firmly gripping mine. This was it—Vegas. The city of bright lights, endless possibilities, and, for me, unforeseen complications.

Gage's team moved with precision, the rhythm of their steps in sync as we made our way toward the waiting SUVs. I spotted his security team immediately—Sigma, looking as imposing as ever, with his broad shoulders and no-nonsense expression. But it wasn't him that made my heart plummet into my stomach; it was the sight of Vince, standing tall and stoic beside one of the vehicles, his eyes scanning the area until they landed on me.

For a split second, I froze, the noise of the bustling airport fading into the background. Vince was supposed to be back in Eastbrook, not here, not in Vegas, where everything was supposed to be easy and carefree. My heart pounded in my chest as a wave of panic washed over me. But I masked it quickly, forcing a smile onto my face as I turned to Gabby, who was already eyeing me with concern.

"Shit. You good?" Gabby's voice was low, but I could hear the underlying worry.

I shook my head. "No."

"Come here," she said, grabbing my arm and pulling me to the side. "Okay, breathe. Just breathe."

My chest was heaving, and I was starting to hyperventilate. "Gabs...w-what the-the fuck is he doing here?"

"I don't know. He's supposed to be back in Eastbrook," she hissed as she rubbed my back. "Shit! Look, it'll be fine. We'll get through this. I'm here. I won't leave your side if you don't want me to. And besides, you know Vince, he's not going to make a scene. He's too professional for that. I do think, though, that you should find some time later to talk to him privately. I know this little trip was supposed to be all fun and shenanigans, but I'm not sure you can just ignore this, V."

She was right, her words grounding, a small thread of logic in the middle of my spinning thoughts. "Yeah, okay," I whispered back, my voice shaky.

"Hey," Gabby squeezed my arm. "It's gonna be fine. I got you."

I nodded, feeling a little more centered. But then Gage, oblivious to the turmoil brewing inside me, grabbed my hand and pulled me toward one of the SUVs. "You're riding with me, gorgeous," he said with that easy confidence that made my heart flutter in a different way.

I cast a quick glance at Gabby, who shot me a supportive look before I allowed myself to be led away. The driver opened the door to the luxury SUV, and Gage guided me inside. His manager was already seated in the back, engrossed in a conversation on his phone. Sigma hopped into the front seat without a word, his presence solid and reassuring. But as I settled next to Gage, I couldn't stop my eyes from drifting to the other SUV, where Vince was climbing into the passenger seat. I wondered what he was thinking. Was he upset?

The ride to the hotel was quiet, too quiet. The plush leather of the seats should have been comforting, but I couldn't shake the feeling of anxiety clawing at my insides. Gage noticed, of course, he did—he always noticed. But instead of pressing me, he just tightened his grip on my hand, pressing a soft kiss to my temple as he tucked me against his side. It was a small gesture, but it was enough to calm my racing thoughts, if only for a moment.

We pulled up to an underground entrance at the MGM Grand, the hotel that was hosting the fight.

My heart raced as we got out of the SUV, and Sigma quickly ushered us inside. Gage's manager, still on his phone, followed behind us. We entered an elevator and went straight up to the penthouse suite.

I looked at Gage questioningly.

"Check-in was already handled. Our bags will be in the room when we get there," he said. "Perks of being the talent," he added with a grin.

The elevator dinged, and the doors slid open, revealing a long hallway with lush carpet. Gage was still holding my hand, and I could feel the heat from his palm seeping into mine, grounding me. But it wasn't enough to stop the nerves from building up again as we exited the elevator and approached the penthouse suite.

Vince was there, stationed outside the door with another guard—a tall, muscular woman with warm brown skin and a serious expression that screamed, 'Don't mess with me.' The faint trace of a scar running from her left eyebrow down to her chin was intriguing, making me want to get to know the woman, certain she had stories upon stories to tell. She gave me a quick, professional nod as we approached, her black eyes sweeping over me with a quick assessment before returning to scan the hallway.

She was interesting, but it was Vince who held my attention. He didn't say a word as we passed, his expression unreadable, but his presence was a solid weight on my shoulders. Gage, who was either pretending not to notice the tension or just ignoring it, nodded at Vince in greeting before leading me into the suite.

The penthouse was nothing short of spectacular —floor-to-ceiling windows with a panoramic view of the strip, plush furnishings in rich tones of gold and cream, and a separate bedroom with a massive bed that looked like it belonged in a palace. But all I could think about was Vince, standing out there in the hallway, and the conversation I knew I would have to have with him.

Gage turned to me as soon as we were alone in the suite. "You good?" he asked, his voice soft, his eyes searching mine.

I forced a smile and nodded. "Yeah, just... tired, I guess. It was kind of a long flight, and long flights make me tired."

He didn't look convinced, but he didn't push it either. Instead, he pulled me into his arms, holding me close as he pressed a kiss to the top of my head. "Why don't you take a bath then lay down? Rest before we meet everyone for dinner. I have to head down and meet with Russ and my team so they can brief me. I should be back in about an hour. Cool?"

I nodded against his chest, letting myself relax into his embrace, if only for a moment.

Gage pulled back and took my hand. He led me

to the large bathroom and proceeded to run me a bath. He squirted a heaping amount of body wash into the water, and it immediately bubbled up. He turned and crooked his finger for me to come over. I did, and he started undressing me as soon as I reached him. The only items he had to remove were my dress and bra since he'd already rid me of my panties earlier. I slipped out of my flats and took his hand as he helped me into the water. It was nice and steamy how I liked it, and the tub was filling up fast. Once I was fully immersed, Gage turned off the water and kneeled next to the tub. He tucked a finger under my chin, lifting my gaze to his.

"Thank you for coming to support me," he said, his voice low and intense.

"Of course. You know I got your back," I told him.

"I appreciate that, and I know with you at my back, I can't lose." He kissed my lips then - softly and sweetly. "Relax. Rest. I'll be back soon." And with that, he left.

As I sank deeper into the steaming bath, the bubbles encasing me in their fragrant warmth, my mind refused to quiet. The tension of the day lingered, a constant, nagging presence at the back of my thoughts. I closed my eyes, trying to focus on the soothing scent of lavender that filled the room, but it was no use. The moment I saw Vince standing outside that SUV, replayed over and over again in my head.

What was he thinking? Did he hate me for parading around with Gage right in front of him? Or worse, was he completely indifferent? That thought, the possibility that seeing me with Gage might have pushed Vince to stop caring at all, sent a fresh wave of anxiety crashing through me.

This love triangle was of my own making—no one else's. I knew that. And yet, I was trapped, unable to figure out how to extricate myself without tearing everything apart. Vince had never really seen me "be with" Gage, and now, here he was, forced to stand by and watch us together. The shit was crazy.

The worst part was that Vince hadn't shown any emotion, hadn't given me even the slightest clue as to what he was thinking or feeling. He'd just stood there, stone-faced and unreadable, while I clung to Gage's hand like it was some kind of lifeline. And now, I was left to wonder whether Vince was bottling up his anger or if he had already checked out emotionally.

The thought of losing Vince—of him deciding he wanted nothing more to do with me—was like a punch to the gut. I couldn't breathe. My heart felt like it was being squeezed in a vice. How did I let it get to this point? I should have been upfront with both of them from the start. Now, I was in a mess so tangled I didn't even know where to begin unraveling it.

With Gage gone to his meeting, the empty penthouse echoed with the silence of my uncertainty. I knew I couldn't keep going like this, pretending everything was fine when it clearly wasn't. I needed to talk to Vince, to find out what he was thinking, even if the conversation led to a place I wasn't ready to go.

But the thought of that conversation terrified me. What if this was the nail in the coffin for us? What if Vince couldn't handle seeing me with Gage and decided he was done, for good? The very idea sent a chill down my spine, one that the heat of the bath couldn't chase away.

I inhaled deeply, the lavender scent mingling with the fear that twisted my stomach. I had to do something. Sitting here, letting my thoughts consume me, wasn't going to solve anything. The decision was made. I stood up, water cascading down my skin, and I reached for one of the fluffy white robes hanging by the tub. The soft fabric wrapped around me like a protective shield as I padded barefoot to the door.

My heart pounded in my chest; each beat a drum of uncertainty. I took a deep breath to calm my nerves, gripping the doorknob as if it might give me the strength I needed. Then, with a shaky exhale, I opened the door.

But instead of Vince, I found a different man standing guard. Tall, lean, and alert, he wasn't the comforting presence I'd hoped for. Vince was gone. Panic flared in my chest. Where was he? Had he left? Was he so upset that he couldn't stand to be near me?

The female guard was still there; she glanced at me, her expression curious. Her presence only intensified my anxiety, but I forced myself to nod in her direction, a silent acknowledgment that I was fine, even if I wasn't.

"Ma'am, is everything alright?" The woman's voice was low and respectful, but the concern was clear.

I shook my head slightly. "Yes, I'm fine. I was umm... just looking..."

"Would you like me to fetch anything for you?" she asked, her eyes searching mine.

"Umm... no. No, thank you," I replied, my voice barely above a whisper. "I umm... I'm gonna get some rest."

She nodded, satisfied with my answer, and I closed the door softly behind me, the click of the latch sounding much louder in the silence of the suite.

I stood there for a moment, staring at the closed door, willing myself to calm down. Where was Vince? I know he didn't just leave. He was probably just out on another detail somewhere else in the hotel. He had a job to do, and he was good at compartmentalizing. But still, the nagging worry gnawed at me, making it impossible to relax.

Finally, I climbed into the massive bed; the sheets cool against my skin. I pulled the blankets up to my chin, trying to find comfort in the plush mattress and the soft pillows that surrounded me. But sleep didn't come easily. My mind kept circling back to Vince, to Gage, to the impossible situation I'd placed myself in.

I stared up at the ceiling, the faint sound of the city buzzing in the distance. My eyelids grew heavy, but my mind remained restless. I couldn't believe this was happening. I knew I'd eventually have to put my big girl panties on and face the music, but for now, I'd rest.

As exhaustion finally began to claim me, I whispered a silent prayer that Vince would understand, that somehow, we could find a way through this mess. But deep down, I wasn't sure if that was even possible.

CHAPTER SIXTEEN

VINCE

The dry desert air hit my face as I stood on the tarmac, the sun casting long shadows over the tarmac. The private jet had just started to taxi toward its spot, and I felt the familiar steadiness settle in my chest. This was routine—security checks and ensuring everything was in proper order. Another day on the job. But I couldn't shake the tension building low in my gut, no matter how hard I tried to focus on the task at hand.

I kept my gaze locked on the jet door as it finally opened, the stairs lowering with a smooth mechanical hum. Gage stepped out first, tall and confident as always. But then she followed, Vanessa, her hand clasped comfortably in his. My breath hitched, but I forced my face to remain impassive, locked in the professional demeanor that was second nature to me. This was the reality I'd known, but seeing it played out in front of me hit harder than I'd expected.

My mind raced, a swirl of emotions that I couldn't quite put into words. I wasn't jealous—

Nah, that wasn't it. But seeing Vanessa with Gage, holding his hand, sharing that quiet, intimate connection out in the open, made it all more real. She looked happy; her smile wide as she laughed at something he said. And damn, that mattered to me more than I wanted to admit.

She had no idea I'd be here, and the shock that covered her face when she saw me was evident in her brown eyes and the stiffness in her body. She looked terrified. I wanted to go to her but I couldn't. Now was not the time or place. So, I forced myself to look away, shaking it off and reminding myself that I was here to work, not to dwell on shit I couldn't control. We started moving toward the SUVs, and I slipped into autopilot, walking with my team, making sure everything was in order for the drive to the hotel. My body went through the motions, but my mind, my mind kept replaying that image—Vanessa, holding his hand, looking at him like he was the most important person in her world.

The SUV engines roared to life, and I caught myself glancing back at the car Vanessa was in with Gage one more time before slipping into my role completely. There was a familiar pang in my chest, but I locked it down. I couldn't allow this situation to interfere with work. Besides, I was Vince-Mutherfucking-Cartwright. I didn't show my hand unless I wanted to.

As we pulled away from the airport, the tension in my gut didn't ease, but I had it in check. And it would remain there.

The MGM Grand was a hive of activity as we arrived, the buzz of the casino floor humming beneath our feet as we made our way through the lobby. The team moved with purpose; our steps synchronized as we headed toward the private elevator that would take us up to the penthouse suite. I kept my eyes forward, mind locked on the job at hand. This was routine—security sweeps, ensuring everything was exactly where it needed to be. But there was an edge to the air today, a tension I couldn't quite shake.

The elevator doors slid open with a soft chime, revealing the corridor that led to the suite. The luxury of the place was apparent from the moment we stepped out—plush carpets underfoot, the walls adorned with expensive artwork that I barely spared a glance at. I was here to do a job, not to admire the décor.

"Alright, team," Sigma's voice cut through the silence as he stepped out first. "Let's make this quick and thorough."

I gave a nod to the guys as we moved through the space, checking every corner and every possible entry point, making sure the security measures were solid. The suite itself was immaculate, as expected—a sprawling space with floor-to-ceiling windows offering a panoramic view of the strip below, a massive king-sized bed in the center of the bedroom, and a living area that screamed luxury.

As we moved from room to room, I forced myself to focus, to push aside the image of Vanessa and Gage stepping off that jet together. I couldn't afford distractions, not now. But damn, it was harder than I thought. Every now and then, the image would slip into my mind, unbidden, and I'd have to push it back down, remind myself of where I was, what I was doing.

I was in the bedroom, checking the balcony doors and ensuring they were secure when the elevator dinged down the hall. My body tensed involuntarily, and I knew without looking who had arrived.

"Vince," Sigma's voice came through the earpiece, calm and collected. "All clear?"

"Yeah, all clear," I replied, my tone even, hiding the way my pulse quickened at the thought of seeing Vanessa again. I stepped out of the bathroom, rejoining the team in the hallway just as the elevator doors opened.

Gage and Vanessa stepped out; their hands still intertwined. My eyes found her immediately—her hair was slightly tousled from the flight, her lips curved in a soft smile as she listened to something Gage was saying. Seeing them again hit me square in the chest, but I didn't flinch. My face remained a mask of calm professionalism as I watched them approach. Gage gave me a nod of acknowledgment, a quick, almost imperceptible gesture.

"Gage, your room's all set," Sigma informed him, his tone strictly business. "There'll be two guards stationed at your door at all times.

"Thanks, man," Gage replied, his voice easy, unaffected. He turned to Vanessa, his hand still gripping hers. "I think you're gonna like this suite," he told her as he pulled her into the suite behind him.

I felt Vanessa's eyes on me for the briefest of moments, a flicker of something in her gaze that I couldn't quite read, before she disappeared inside. The door closed behind them with a soft click, and I forced myself to exhale, releasing the breath I hadn't realized I was holding. The tension in my chest eased just a fraction, but the unease lingered, a stark reminder that this wasn't just another normal job.

"Vince," Sigma's voice broke through my thoughts, pulling me back to the present. He was standing by the door, watching me with that knowing look of his. "Let's go meet with hotel security. We need to make sure everything's squared away for this weekend's activities."

"Sure," I said, forcing myself to move, to fall back into the rhythm of the job. "Let's do it."

As we made our way down the hall, I focused on the task at hand, compartmentalizing everything else. I was here to do a job and nothing—no matter how much it twisted me up inside—was going to get in the way of that.

The security briefing with the hotel staff was efficient and straightforward. We went over every detail, from emergency exits to pre-fight events to the schedule for fight night, making sure nothing was left to chance. I was in my element here, in control, running through scenarios and solutions with a calm, measured approach.

But even as we wrapped up the meeting and Sigma clapped me on the shoulder, telling me I had the rest of the night off, the tension in my chest didn't ease. It stayed with me, a silent companion, as I walked out of the conference room and headed toward one of the hotel bars.

I needed a drink. I needed to clear my head. But more than anything, I needed to figure out how the hell I was going to deal with this weekend without ruining things for and with Vanessa.

The hotel bars weren't giving the vibe I needed so I head down to Old Vegas. I found a small bar back in the cut-down on Fremont Street. The bar was dimly lit, the kind of place where the shadows seemed to hold secrets, and the soft glow of the amber lights made everything look a little more golden, a little more timeless. The clinking of glasses and low hum of conversations filled the air, creating a background noise that was almost comforting. It was the perfect place to get lost in your thoughts, which was exactly what I needed.

I settled into a stool at the far end of the bar, away from the main crowd. The leather was worn, the kind of seat that had seen countless nights and even more stories. I signaled the bartender, who nodded in acknowledgment before sliding a glass of whiskey toward me. I took a slow sip, letting the warmth of the liquor spread through my chest, grounding me in the present, even as my mind kept drifting back to earlier in the day.

Seeing Vanessa with Gage, out in the open like that, had been... a lot. More than I expected it to be. Not jealousy, but something close, something that gnawed at the edges of my thoughts, no matter how much I tried to shake it off. I knew the deal with Vanessa. We weren't official in the sense that we defined what we were doing, but she was mine, and I was hers, and we both knew that. I also knew that she was Gage's too. I just never had to see it so fully before. I needed to sit with that.

I was so lost in my thoughts that I didn't notice E slip onto the stool next to me until she ordered her drink. She didn't say anything at first, just nodded to the bartender, who poured her a whiskey neat. The silence between us was comfortable, familiar, the kind that didn't need filling.

In the short time that I'd known E, I'd learned that at times she could be quiet but sharp, always observing, always reading the room. She didn't strike me as the prying type, but I could feel her eyes on me, assessing, waiting.

After a few moments, she finally broke the silence, her voice low and calm. "You good?"

I glanced at her, taking in her steady gaze and the way she swirled the whiskey in her glass before taking a sip. There was no judgment in her black eyes, just a genuine concern that threw me off guard.

"Yeah," I said, though it lacked any real conviction.

She nodded as if expecting that response. "You sure? Your energy's been a little off today. I know I haven't known you that long, but I read people. Read you the first time we met in person. And this version of you," she waved a hand at me, "Is not the norm. Wanna talk about it?"

I hesitated, swirling my own drink as I weighed my options. E was sharp—she wouldn't have approached me if she didn't already have a read on the situation. So, I decided to skip the bullshit.

"It's Vanessa. We have a... a thing back home," I admitted.

E's expression didn't change, but there was a flicker of understanding in her eyes. "Yeah, I figured as much. I saw the way you kept trying not to watch her and the way she kept cutting her eyes at you. She was looking for you earlier, you know? She came to the door after Gage left for his meeting. I think she was hoping you'd be there."

That caught me off guard. "Really?"

"Yeah," E confirmed, taking another sip of her whiskey. "If you ask me, she's just as twisted up about this as you are."

I sighed, running a hand over my jaw. "Probably. She didn't know I was gonna be here."

E's brow lifted. "Why didn't you tell her?"

I shrugged. "I don't know. I guess I didn't want to ruin her trip." I took a swig of my drink. "I don't know. It's complicated what we have. It's like... we're together, but it's not official. I don't tell her who to see, and she don't tell me. When we're together, we're together. It's not like we hide it. It's just..."

"Complicated. I know." E set her glass down, turning to face me fully. "Look, Vince, I'm not trying to get all up in your shit, but you seem to really like this woman. And from what I observed, she has mad feelings for you as well. But she also clearly cares deeply for Gage. And Gage obviously knows about you two, so what I'm saying is, this situation is only complicated because ya'll making it that way. You three need to have a conversation."

I just stared at her, wondering what kind of skillset she had that allowed her to read exactly what was going on between me, Vanessa, and Gage. I watched as she drained the last of her whiskey, the amber liquid disappearing in one smooth motion. She set the glass down with a soft clink, her movements deliberate and measured, as if she was weighing the gravity of what she'd just said.

She caught my eye, and I swear, it felt like she was looking straight through me. "Don't try to figure me out," she said, her voice calm but laced with something deeper, something darker. "I gotta a long history and a lot of secrets."

With that, she stood, pulling a few bills from her pocket, and tossing them onto the bar without a second glance. "Have a good night, Vince," she added, her tone final, like she knew she'd said everything that needed to be said.

I watched her walk out of the bar, her silhouette disappearing into the twinkling lights of Freemont Street. For a long moment, I just sat there, staring at the empty glass in front of me, E's words bouncing around in my head like a pinball. She'd seen right through me; through the cool exterior I was trying so damn hard to maintain. The ease with which she'd done it left me both impressed and unnerved.

I signaled to the bartender for another drink, but as he poured, I knew it wouldn't do much to quiet the storm raging in my mind. E was right.

This whole situation was complicated because we were making it complicated. Vanessa was caught up in it just as much as I was. Maybe more. I took a sip of the whiskey, letting it burn down my throat, but the heat didn't ease the tension in my chest.

I knew what I had to do. E's words had been the push I needed, the jolt to snap me out of my own head. This couldn't go on like this—not for Vanessa, not for me, and not for Gage. Whatever was going to happen between the three of us needed to be out in the open. No more guessing, no more hiding behind professional walls and unspoken boundaries. The moment this fight was over, it was time to confront this head-on.

I didn't know how the conversation with Vanessa would go. Hell, I didn't even know what I was going to say. But I knew it was time. Time to stop running from this, from us, from whatever the hell this was going to turn into. It was time to deal, no matter the outcome.

CHAPTER SEVENTEEN

VANESSA

The early morning light filtered through the curtains of the penthouse suite, casting a soft, golden hue across the room. I stared at the ceiling, the weight of the previous day pressing heavily on my chest. The tension between Vince and me was like a tight knot that refused to unravel, no matter how much I tried to push it aside. I had barely slept, my mind replaying every glance, every missed opportunity to talk to him.

I rolled over in bed, feeling the empty space beside me where Gage had been earlier. He was already up, his familiar routine playing out in the background as he did his morning exercises —push-ups, sit-ups, the rhythmic sounds of his movement steady and reassuring. I watched him for a moment, admiring the way his muscles moved under his skin, his focus unshakable. Gage was in his zone, completely locked into his mini-workout.

Part of me wanted to just roll over and go back

to sleep, to avoid everything for just a little while longer. But that wasn't an option. Not today. I needed to find a way to talk to Vince, to explain myself, to somehow make things right before it all spiraled out of control. Who was I kidding? Things were already out of control.

I pushed the covers back and slid out of bed, the plush carpet soft against my bare feet as I padded across the room. Gage noticed me and offered a small smile as he finished another set of push-ups, wiping the sweat from his brow with a towel.

"Morning, gorgeous," he said, his voice warm but tinged with concern. "You good? You were pretty restless last night - tossing and turning."

I forced a smile, trying to hide the unease that had settled deep in my gut. "I'm okay. Sorry about last night. I hope I didn't keep you up. You need your rest. And don't you have a really intense training session later today? Shit! If you lose the fight, it's gonna be my fault," I fretted, the words tumbling out before I could stop them.

Gage's expression softened, and he was by my side in an instant, pulling me against his chest. His touch was comforting, his strength something I could lean on. He tucked a finger under my chin, lifting my gaze to meet his. His lids lowered, and he pulled his bottom lip between his teeth. He stared down at me. "You so damn cute when you being extra," he said, and I scrunched my nose up at him.

"I'm not extra," I pouted.

He chuckled, and the sound rumbled through his chest right into me. "Oh, gorgeous, you and I both know how extra you can be."

"Whatever!" I spat and pretended to try and pull away from him.

Gage tightened his grip around my waist and buried his face in my neck. He ran his nose along the column of my neck up to my ear before lapping at it, catching my earlobe between his teeth, and gently nibbling.

I melted into him and tilted my head, giving him all the access he wanted.

"Couple things," he whispered against my ear. "First, I slept fine. Yeah, you were tossing and turning a bit, but once I wrapped you up in my arms, you were good. Second, I told you I don't lose. Third, you're lucky I'm on my celibate shit for this fight. Otherwise, I'd bend your lil extra ass over and fuck the shit outta that tight little pussy."

My stomach tightened, and my pussy instantly started leaking. "Don't be saying shit like that when you know good and well you can't fuck me right now," I whined.

He just laughed and pulled me back against him, squeezing me tightly. "I'm so glad you're here, V," he said. "I mean that."

I bit into my cheek to stop the tears pricking at

the back of my eyes. Okay, maybe Gage was right; I might be a little extra. But I had to cut myself some slack; things were crazy for me right now. I pulled back a bit and stared up at him. "I'm glad to be here supporting you. Thank you for inviting me," I told him, then lifted up on my toes and pressed my lips to his.

The moment our lips touched, something electric sparked between us. Desire coursed through my veins, hot like liquid fire, fueled by the softness of his mouth on mine. His hands tightened around my waist as he deepened the kiss, taking control in the way he knew best, his strong, sure moves making me weak in the knees. His tongue slipped into my mouth effortlessly, exploring every corner with an erotic finesse that made me sway against him.

Every fiber of my body ached for him, ached for the heat his touch promised. His lips were firm yet succulent as they moved against mine in an intoxicating rhythm; his tongue was bold and unapologetic, adding fuel to the fire already consuming me. My hands found their way up his chest, clutching at him like a lifeline as he continued to dominate my senses with his taste. The hint of mint laced with something earthy and purely Gage was intoxicating.

My pulse hammered in my ears, each thump mirroring the rising tide of my desire. Gage's hands left my waist, sliding down to cup my ass, his grip firm, pulling me flush against him. I could feel him, hard and heavy against my stomach, and a small whimper escaped me at the tantalizing promise of what lay beneath those gym shorts.

He broke the kiss abruptly, his breathing as ragged as mine, his dark eyes smoldering with a lust that mirrored my own. "Fuck! I want you so bad, V," he muttered under his breath, dropping his forehead to rest on mine. His words sent a delicious shiver down my spine, and I closed my eyes against the onslaught.

Gage released me and stepped back, his eyes heavy-lidded and dark with desire. His gaze held mine captive as he slowly licked his lips, tasting the last remnants of the molten kiss we had shared. His chest was heaving, each ragged breath a testament to the effort it was taking him to resist the temptation I presented.

"Go and shower, Vanessa," he commanded in a husky voice that vibrated with barely suppressed hunger. "Before I fuck up my whole celibacy shit and bend your ass over right here."

I could only nod in response, too caught up in the whirlwind of desire that was sweeping through me to find my voice. I turned on shaky legs and walked towards the bathroom, feeling his searing gaze burning into my back every step of the way.

Once inside, I rested my forehead against the cool tiles of the shower wall, inhaling deeply in an attempt to steady myself. The contrast between the cold tiles and the hot water was soothing. I let it cascade down my back, washing away the tension that had knotted in my muscles. A feeling of raw vulnerability washed over me as images of Gage's smoldering gaze scorched through my mind, followed by Vince's questioning eyes.

I blew out a breath. I needed to talk to Vince - today. I didn't want to let another day; another moment go by in this hotbox of tension. Resolved, I quickly finished my shower and headed back into the bedroom to get dressed.

Gage was no longer in the bedroom, so I was able to get dressed without distraction. I pulled on a simple black mini-dress and made my way into the living area, where Gage's team was already gathering for breakfast. The smell of coffee and pastries filled the air, but I barely noticed as my eyes immediately sought out Vince. He was across the room, deep in conversation with Sigma, his expression all business as they discussed security measures for the day.

I scanned the room for Gage but didn't see him.

"He's in the guest bathroom showering," Gabby whispered behind me, and I whipped around to face her.

"I wasn't-"

She reached out and squeezed my shoulder, silencing me. "Don't even try to deny it. I know you, friend. You've been on edge ever since we got off that plane and you saw Vince. I know you want to talk to him."

I sighed. "I do. I need to talk to him, Gabby. I have no idea what he's thinking about Gage and me, me and him. Hell, what does he feel about us after seeing me with Gage?" I panicked.

Gabby ran a soothing hand up and down my arm. "Panicking won't help. Look, on some level, Vince already knew about you and Gage, so he can't be too surprised that you're here. I agree you two need to talk; you'll just have to do it later."

"I know. You're right. Besides, today is going to be crazy busy with all the pre-fight events. I'll wait until later," I said. "Did you already get food?" I asked her.

"Not yet."

"Well, come eat with me and help keep my mind off my dramatic-ass love life." I grabbed her hand and pulled her to the breakfast spread that had been set up.

We ate and quietly chatted while Gage and his team discussed the day's events.

***

The conference room at the MGM Grand was buzzing with energy. Cameras flashed, reporters murmured among themselves, and Gage's name was on everyone's lips. The fight was the event of the weekend, and the press conference had drawn a significant crowd. I sat in the front row with Gabby and Griff, trying to focus on the event, but my mind kept drifting to the side of the room where Vince was stationed.

From where I sat, I could see Vince standing near the door, his expression unreadable as he scanned the room. Even in a crowd, he had a presence that was hard to ignore—steadfast, reliable, and always on alert. But right now, all I wanted was to get a moment alone with him, to explain... to... I don't even know what exactly. Something.

Gage, meanwhile, was handling the press with his usual charm and confidence, answering questions with a grin that made the reporters eat out of the palm of his hand. He was in his element, completely at ease in front of the cameras. I tried to match his energy, plastering a supportive smile on my face as I watched him speak, but my thoughts kept drifting back to Vince.

The press conference was long, much longer than I'd expected, and with each passing minute, my anxiety grew. I needed to talk to Vince before this got any more complicated than it already was. Finally, I said fuck it and told Gabby I was running to the ladies room.

I stood up, careful not to draw too much

attention to myself, and made my way toward the back of the room where Vince was now. My heart pounded in my chest as I got closer to Vince. But just as I was about to reach him, I felt a hand on my arm, pulling me aside.

"Vanessa, a quick word?" It was Gage's manager, his tone polite but firm, making it clear this wasn't optional. I bit back my frustration and turned to face him, forcing a smile.

"Of course," I replied, trying to keep my voice even.

He led me a few steps away from the crowd, away from Vince. He began discussing the logistics for the weigh-in and pre-fight dinner happening later that night, saying Gage wanted to make sure I was okay with standing with his team at the weigh-in, knowing it would be blasted on TV and social media. I nodded along, trying to stay focused on what he was saying, but my eyes kept flicking back to Vince, whose attention was fixed on the crowd, ever vigilant.

"As for tonight's dinner," his manager continued, "Gage asked that you sit with him at the head of the table. It's not the norm for him to have a woman at these things. Must mean you're important to him."

The comment caught me off guard, and I blinked, trying to process what he was implying. "Oh, uh... I didn't realize," I stammered, unsure of what to say.

He smiled, a knowing look in his eyes. "You're the first woman he's invited to be a part of his fight weekend, so it's safe to say he really likes you. A lot."

I managed to nod, my mind spinning. The pressure of the situation was starting to feel like a physical weight on my shoulders, and the reminder of how much I meant to Gage only added to my confusion. I needed to talk to Vince to sort this out before it consumed me.

"Thank you," I finally said, hoping my voice didn't betray the turmoil inside me.

Gage's manager gave me a nod and walked off to deal with another matter, leaving me standing there, staring at the spot where Vince had been just moments ago. But now, he was gone, already moving with Sigma to secure Gage's exit. Another missed opportunity. Another chance to talk to Vince slipped through my fingers.

I let out a frustrated sigh. The press conference was wrapping up, and I could see Gage making his way toward the exit, surrounded by his entourage. I was about to follow when Gabby appeared beside me, giving me a curious look.

"You good?" she asked, her voice laced with concern.

I nodded, forcing another smile. "Yeah. Yeah... no. You know I'm not. I keep trying to get a minute with Vince, but I can't seem to."

Gabby raised an eyebrow, her lips curving into a sympathetic smile. "I figured as much. You've been on edge all morning."

I sighed, feeling the weight of the situation pressing down on me even more. "I just keep missing my chance, Gabby. I need to talk to him, but every time I try, something or someone gets in the way. It's like the universe is against me right now."

Gabby glanced over her shoulder at the commotion as Gage and his team made their way out of the conference room. "You know what? Screw lunch with the group. Let's ditch it and go have some girl time. We can hit the Strip, do some shopping, grab a drink—anything to get your mind off all this for a little while. What do you say?"

I blinked, surprised by her suggestion, but relief quickly washed over me. "You know what? That sounds like exactly what I need."

Gabby grinned and linked her arm with mine, leading me away from the hustle and bustle of the press conference. "Come on, let's get out of here before someone tries to rope us into more plans."

"Don't you want to tell Griff-"

She cut me off. "I'll text him. Let's go."

As we slipped out of the conference room and into the bustling hallway, I felt a small sense of freedom, like I was finally able to breathe again. The tension in my shoulders began to ease as we walked through the hotel lobby and out into the warm Vegas sunshine.

"First stop?" Gabby asked as we strolled toward the Strip, the excitement in her voice contagious. "Shopping or drinks?"

"Definitely drinks," I replied with a genuine smile, already feeling lighter.

Gabby laughed, the sound bright and carefree. "Oh, I'm with that. I want one of those slushy drinks I've been seeing folks walk around with."

As we walked down the Strip, arm in arm, I let myself relax, if only for a little while. I knew the situation with Vince would still be there when I got back, but for now, I had Gabby, the vibrant energy of Vegas, and a few hours to forget about everything else. And that was more than enough.

CHAPTER EIGHTEEN

GAGE

The arena was alive with the kind of energy you could only find in Vegas. The noise was a relentless buzz, a mixture of excited fans, camera flashes, and the murmur of journalists talking into their microphones. It was a scene I'd lived through countless times before, but this time, it felt different—more intense, more charged.

I walked through the tunnel with my team, Sigma leading the way and Vince not far behind, his eyes constantly scanning, always alert. The lights were bright, the air thick with anticipation. I could feel the adrenaline already starting to pump through my veins, that familiar rush of excitement and focus. This was where I thrived, where I was meant to be. But even as I stepped into the arena, taking in the crowd, the flashing cameras, and the massive banners with my face on them, my mind was somewhere else.

Or rather, with someone else.

I spotted her almost immediately—Vanessa. She was standing off to the side with Gabby and Griff, looking as stunning as ever, but there was a tension in her posture that I couldn't ignore. Her smile was there, but it didn't quite reach her eyes. I knew her well enough to recognize that she was putting on a brave face. The sight of Vince stationed near the stage, his face all business, didn't help. I knew he was just doing his job, but the dynamic between the three of us was starting to wear on her. Hell, it was starting to wear on me too.

But I pushed those thoughts aside, forcing myself to focus. I had a job to do. The weigh-in was just a formality, something I could do in my sleep, but it was important. It was a part of the ritual, a part of getting into the right headspace for the fight. I couldn't afford to be distracted—not now.

I made my way to the scale, blocking out the noise, the lights, the people. It was just me and the task at hand. The moment I stepped onto the scale, I was locked in. The announcer's voice boomed through the speakers, calling out my stats for the world to hear. The crowd erupted, cheering my name, but it all felt distant, like it was happening in another world.

Then came the stare down. I locked eyes with my opponent, my expression hard, unyielding. I could feel the intensity in the air, the crowd feeding off it, but my thoughts kept flickering back to Vanessa. I wondered if she was watching, if she could see the conflict I was trying so hard to hide. I couldn't let it show. Not here.

After what felt like an eternity, the pomp and grandeur of the weigh-in came to an end. I stepped off the scale, my heart still pounding, but for entirely different reasons. I scanned the room, searching for Vanessa again. When I found her, she was looking right at me, her eyes soft but full of something I couldn't quite place. Worry? Fear? Maybe both.

I gave her a small nod, hoping it conveyed what I couldn't say out loud—that we'd talk, that I'd make sure she was okay, but later. Right now, I needed to stay focused.

Reporters shouted questions at me, but I ignored them and walked the short distance to where Vanessa stood with Gabby and Griff. I quickly dapped up Griff, kissed Gabby on the cheek, and then pulled Vanessa to me, feeling the warmth of her body against mine.

"Hey, gorgeous," I whispered against her ear.

She smiled up at me, but it was a shadow of her usual one. "Hey, handsome. You looked good up there. That Damien Fields is a big muthafucka, though. Be careful tonight."

I grinned, liking that she was worried about me. "Like my grandmother used to say, the bigger they are, the harder they fall. That nigga's bout to taste the ring floor."

Her smile widened, reaching her eyes now, and

that made my chest expand. I liked seeing her genuinely happy. "You ready to be my personal cheerleader tonight?"

"Of course. I got you," she said. Her gaze turned serious. "How are you doing, really?"

"I'm good. This is what I do. I just want to make sure you're okay. I know it's a lot, and... you not used to all this press and shit."

She cupped my cheek. "You're right. It's a lot, but I'm... dealing. I just want to be here for you and support you the way you need me to. I don't want to be a distraction."

"Trust me, you not. I want you here, V," I told her, then placed a soft kiss on her forehead.

She nodded, her eyes searching mine for something. Reassurance, maybe. Or just confirmation that I meant what I said. I squeezed her waist gently, then let go, turning back to face the crowd, my game face back on.

The weigh-in was over in a flash after that, just a blur of handshakes, quick photos, and more noise than I cared to deal with. As soon as I could, I started moving towards the exit, Vanessa by my side. My security team already in motion, ensuring everything was secure and clearing the path for us. I caught Vince's eye as we moved, and for a moment, something unspoken passed between us. We both knew this situation was precarious, but we also knew it wasn't something we could afford to address right now.

There would be time for that later.

For now, the fight was the priority. And nothing —not even the complicated mess that was brewing between Vanessa, Vince, and me—was going to get in the way of that.

The adrenaline from the weigh-in was still coursing through my veins as we made our way back to the hotel. The ride was quiet, filled with a comfortable silence that let me focus on what was ahead. I kept my arm wrapped around Vanessa, her presence grounding me even as my thoughts swirled with the fight strategies and the press obligations still to come.

By the time we arrived back at the MGM Grand, the sun had started to set, casting the strip in a warm, golden glow. The city was waking up, getting ready for the night, just like I was. I had one more event to get through before I could truly lock in—dinner with the team. It was a tradition, something we did before every fight. A way to unwind just a little before the storm hit.

As soon as we stepped out of our suite, Sigma was there. His expression was unreadable, as always, but I knew he had everything under control. He gave me a brief nod before falling into step behind us, his presence as solid as ever. Vince was waiting at the elevator. I could feel him watching as we approached. I couldn't front; he was good at this personal security shit. Since we'd got here, he'd been alert and super watchful, even with everything going on. I appreciated that about him.

Per my team's request, we took the regular elevators down to the casino floor as opposed to the service elevators we'd been using. It was the norm for us to make a bit of a scene before fight night by walking through the casino to help generate buzz. We were recognized immediately as we made our way through the hotel, the buzz of the casino floor rising and falling around us. The bright lights, the sound of slot machines, the laughter—it was all a backdrop to what was coming. Vanessa stayed close to me, her hand tightening around mine as we moved through the crowd. People waved, and some even approached for autographs. Not everyone liked the whole crowd engagement thing, but I didn't mind it. I enjoyed interacting with my fans or just boxing fans in general.

When we got to the private dining room, it was already set up. The long table was draped in crisp white linen, the place settings immaculate, and the soft light from the chandeliers above gave the room a warm, intimate feel. My team was already gathering, the conversation light and full of anticipation for what was coming.

I guided Vanessa to the seat next to mine at

the head of the table, pulling out her chair before taking my own. As soon as we sat down, the waitstaff started moving, pouring wine, bringing out appetizers—everything designed to make this as smooth and enjoyable as possible. It was nice, but my mind was elsewhere.

I glanced around the table, taking in the faces of the people who were there to support me. Griff was on the other side of the table, already deep in conversation with Gabby, his hand resting on hers as they spoke quietly. My manager was to my left, going over last-minute details with one of the trainers, their voices low but intense. And then there was Vince, standing near the entrance with Sigma, both of them watching, making sure everything was secure.

Vanessa was quiet beside me, her focus more on the glass of wine in front of her than on the conversation. I reached over and took her hand, squeezing it gently. "You okay?" I asked, my voice low so that only she could hear.

She looked up at me, her eyes meeting mine. There was a flicker of something in her gaze— uncertainty, maybe. Or fear. "Yeah," she replied after a moment, her voice steady. "I'm fine."

But I knew better. I could feel the tension radiating off her, the way her body was just a little too still, a little too rigid. How quiet she was when she was normally loud, cracking jokes and laughing. The shit fucked with me. I wanted to pull her aside, to tell her that we'd work through this together, but I couldn't do that now. Not with everything else that was going on. I couldn't open up that can of worms before the fight and distract from why we're here.

The waitstaff started bringing out the main course, and the conversation around the table picked up, becoming more animated. Everyone was talking about the fight, about what to expect, about how tonight was going to be a celebration, no matter what. But even as I tried to focus on the conversation, my mind kept drifting back to Vanessa and the elephant in the room.

Vince's presence didn't help either. Every time I glanced his way, he was watching, which is what he should be doing, but fuck! I could see the way Vanessa's eyes kept flicking toward him and could feel the way she was trying to keep it together.

Dinner dragged on, the food and drink flowing freely, and I did my best to enjoy it. Finally, the plates were cleared, and the conversation began to wind down. The energy in the room shifted, and the anticipation for the fight started to build again. I stood up, raising my glass for a toast. The room quieted, all eyes on me.

"To the team," I said, my voice steady. "To everyone who's here tonight, to everyone who's been with me through this journey. We've got a big night ahead of us. We worked hard, and I know we're ready for it. Let's get us another belt."

There was a chorus of cheers and clinking glasses, and I smiled, feeling the support of everyone around me. But as I glanced down at Vanessa, I could see the worry still etched in her features, could feel the tension still simmering beneath the surface.

As the dinner wrapped up and everyone started to disperse, I knew I needed to take a moment. I leaned down, pressing a quick kiss to Vanessa's temple. "Go on up to the suite," I murmured. "I'll be up in a minute."

She nodded, her expression softening just a bit. "Okay."

I watched as she left with Gabby, their figures disappearing through the door. The room began to empty, and soon, it was just me, Sigma, and Vince left. I lingered for a moment, staring at the empty table, my mind racing with everything that still needed to be said, everything that still needed to be resolved.

Finally, I let out a slow breath and turned to Sigma and Vince. "I'm going to head up."

"Vince will escort you up," Sigma said.

I gave him a nod, then headed for the door, Vince on my heels, but a decent distant away. As I made my way to the elevator, the weight of the evening settled on my shoulders. The fight was tomorrow, but it wasn't the only battle I had to face. There were things I needed to confront, conversations I needed to have—things that went far beyond the ring.

***

The crowd's roar filled the arena, a cacophony of sound that seemed to shake the very walls. The energy was electric, the air thick with anticipation. I stood in my corner, rolling my shoulders, feeling the weight of the gloves, the tightness of the tape around my wrists. My heartbeat was steady and controlled, a stark contrast to the chaos around me. This was my world, where everything made sense, where everything was simple: it was win or lose, fight or flight.

My gaze swept over the sea of faces, all of them blending into one mass of expectation. But then, like a magnet, my eyes found Vanessa. She was sitting with Gabby and Griff, her expression a mix of tension and determination. I knew she was worried, not just about the fight but about everything that had led us to this moment. But seeing her there, supporting me, gave me the final piece of focus I needed.

The bell rang, snapping me back to the present. My opponent moved in fast, but I was faster. I dodged his first jab, countering with a swift hook that caught him off guard. The crowd erupted, the noise drowning out everything else. My body moved on autopilot, every muscle and every movement honed from years of training. There was no room for doubt, no room for hesitation. Every punch I threw was calculated; every step deliberate.

But even as I fought, a part of my mind wandered. I thought about Vanessa, about the unexpected and complicated situation we found ourselves in this weekend.

A sharp pain brought me back to the moment— a punch I hadn't seen coming landed squarely on my jaw. I shook it off, my focus snapping back into place. I couldn't afford to be distracted. Not now.

I pushed forward, landing a series of blows that backed my opponent into the ropes. The crowd was on its feet, and the noise was a deafening roar that fueled my adrenaline. I could feel the end coming, the shift in the fight that told me victory was within reach. With one final, powerful uppercut, I sent my opponent crashing to the mat. The ref started the count, but I knew it was over.

The bell rang, signaling the end of the fight. I stood there for a moment, letting it sink in. The crowd went wild, chanting my name, their energy a surge of pure euphoria. I raised my gloves, a grin splitting my face as the ref grabbed my arm and held it up in victory.

The post-fight interviews were a blur, and as

soon as they were over, I made my way to Vanessa, who was dressed in a very short, very tight, very fuckable looking green dress. Shit! she looked good as fuck. I weaved through the throngs of people congratulating me, their voices a blur in the background. All I cared about was getting to her. When I finally reached her, I didn't hesitate—I pulled her into my arms, kissing her hard, right there in front of everyone. It didn't matter who was watching; all that mattered was that she was here, sharing this moment with me.

She kissed me back, her arms wrapping around my neck, and for a second, everything else faded away. It was just us, lost in the aftermath of the fight, in the rush of victory.

When we finally broke apart, I kept her close, my arm around her waist, and looked out at the crowd. That's when I saw him—Vince. He was standing near the edge of the ring, watching us with that same calm expression. No anger, no jealousy, just... acceptance.

I turned back to Vanessa, brushing a stray lock of hair behind her ear. "Let's get out of here," I whispered. "Time to show the fuck out."

The club was everything you'd expect from a Vegas VIP spot—loud music, flashing lights, and a crowd that was more than ready to party. We had our own section, roped off and guarded, but it didn't stop the energy from seeping in. It was infectious, and I found myself caught up in it, the adrenaline from the fight still pumping through my veins.

I kept Vanessa close, my hand on her waist or her thigh, needing that physical connection. Every now and then, I'd lean in, whispering things in her ear that made her blush and laugh. But there was always that edge, that reminder of what I wanted now that the fight was over.

"I can't wait to get you back to the room," I murmured, my lips brushing against her ear. "Remember what you said about losers? Guess who's wearing the belt tonight, sweetheart?"

She looked up at me, her eyes glazed with a mix of alcohol and arousal. "Gage..." she whispered, her voice laced with both excitement and nervousness.

I grinned, pulling her closer. "Nah, lil momma. You was talking mad shit when we was back in Eastbrook. It's time for the champ to get his real prize."

Without another word, I pulled her into me and kissed her—deep. She gripped my shoulders, her nails digging into the fabric of my shirt, and returned the kiss with equal fervor. I felt every ounce of her need, her desire for me. It was intoxicating.

We were breathless when we pulled back, and I could see in the depths of her eyes, the rapid rise and fall of her chest, and the hard way that she swallowed; she was ready. Yeah, she was ready, but I knew she was still caught up about Vince because even in her aroused state, her eyes darted around, looking for him.

The fight was over - I'd won. Now, it was time to win my girl completely by helping her understand that I belonged to her, that she belonged to me, and that we belonged together, no matter what.

"You ready to get out of here," I whispered against her ear, and she nodded. "Say bye to Gabby while I go let Sigma know we ready to bounce."

I moved to the perimeter of the VIP section to where Sigma stood stoic and alert. "Say, man. We ready to head out, me and Vanessa."

"I'll call the car. E will escort ya'll back," he said.

"Bet," I said, then dapped him up.

I made my way back over to Vanessa, who was hugging Gabby. I moved over to Griff and held my hand out to him. He gripped it and pulled me in for a hug, pounding me on the back.

"Ya'll out?" Griff asked.

"Yeah," I yelled over the music. "Time to end this celibacy shit."

Griff's brow lifted, and he chuckled. "Oh, bruh, I know you bout to be wild. Don't have my lil sis out here barely able to walk tomorrow," he joked.

I laughed. "Shit! You can count on that, my nigga."

"Gage!" Gabby called, pushing between me and Griff. She wrapped her thin arms around my neck and pulled me into a hug. "I'm so proud of you. Congrats, champ."

"Thanks, Gabby," I replied, leaning back and staring down at her.

She beamed up at me, then lifted onto her toes to whisper in my ear. "Take care of my girl. She's a lil twisted up right now, but she cares about you. You mean so much to her. I hope you know that."

I tightened my arms around her. "I know," I whispered before placing a soft kiss on the side of Gabby's temple. "You're a good friend."

I released Gabby and then turned to Vanessa. "Ready?" I asked, and she nodded. "Let's go," I said, taking her hand and leading her out of the section. E met us at the opening, and we followed her out.

CHAPTER NINETEEN

VANESSA

The car ride back to the MGM Grand was quiet, the kind of quiet that hummed with unspoken words and lingering energy. The streets of Vegas blurred by in a wash of neon lights, but inside the car, it felt like time had slowed, trapping us in a bubble of intimacy and charged emotions. Gage had his arm around me, his body warm and solid against mine. Every few minutes, he'd press a soft kiss to my temple or the top of my head, each touch sending little sparks of electricity through my skin.

I should have been focused on the present, on Gage and the victory he'd just secured, but my mind was a whirlwind. The day had been intense, more so than I'd expected. Being with Gage, watching him in the ring, feeling the raw power he exuded as he fought—it had all stirred something deep inside me, something that wanted to claim him as mine.

But then there was Vince. No matter how much I tried to push him out of my thoughts, he kept creeping back in. I kept seeing his face in my mind, his steady gaze watching Gage and me during the fight, the way he'd been there, always on the periphery yet somehow central to everything. It was confusing, this tangle of emotions. I felt like I was being pulled in two different directions, and no matter how much I wanted to just be in the moment with Gage, Vince's presence was like a shadow, hovering at the edges of my thoughts, and I knew it was because of how this weekend went down. I had no idea he'd be there working security, and if he knew, he didn't tell me. Why? I had so many questions.

I shifted slightly in my seat, trying to push the conflicting emotions aside. Gage's hand tightened around my waist, pulling me closer. I looked up at him, and he gave me a small, reassuring smile, his eyes soft in the dim light of the car. He wasn't saying anything, but his touch, the way he held me, was enough. It grounded me and gave me something solid to hold on to in the midst of my mental chaos.

I sighed softly, leaning my head against his shoulder. I needed to talk to Vince. I knew that. I couldn't keep avoiding it, couldn't keep letting this unresolved tension simmer under the surface. I had to clear the air, to figure out what was happening between the three of us before it drove me crazy. But not tonight. Tonight, I was with

Gage, and I wanted to focus on him, on us. I'd deal with everything else in the morning.

So, I let myself get lost in the warmth of Gage's body, in the quiet comfort of being close to him. The city outside the window was a blur, but inside the car, everything felt calm, almost peaceful. I let out a slow breath, letting go of the tension that had been knotting in my chest all day.

We pulled into the private, underground parking at the MGM Grand, and as the car rolled to a stop, I felt a strange mix of anticipation and nervousness. I knew where tonight was headed, knew what Gage had in mind. And despite everything else swirling in my head, I wanted it. Wanted him. I glanced up at him again, and the look in his eyes told me he was on the same page.

He helped me out of the car, his hand warm and reassuring around mine as we followed E into the hotel. The long tunnel leading to the elevator bank was quiet, a stark contrast to the chaos of earlier in the night. The elevator ride up to the penthouse was quick, the silence between us thick with unspoken promises. My belly tightened as we reached our floor in anticipation of seeing Vince. But, when the doors slid open, there were two different guards in front of our suite. I was curious as to where Vince was, but I let out a quiet sigh of relief at not having to face him before heading into the suite to get my back blown out by Gage.

The suite was dimly lit, the only light

coming from the floor-to-ceiling windows. It was breathtaking, but all I could focus on was the man beside me, the way his fingers brushed against mine as we walked further into the room. The air felt charged, heavy with the anticipation of what was to come.

The moment we stepped into the suite, I could feel the weight of the night starting to lift, replaced by something else—something heavier, more charged. I looked at Gage. He was already peeling off his jacket, his eyes dark with intent as they locked onto mine.

"I need to shower," I said, my voice hushed, barely above a whisper. "Get all this sweat and smoke off me."

Gage's lips curved into a slow, knowing smile. "A shower sounds good."

I nodded, biting my lip as I took a step toward the bathroom. Gage followed, his presence a comforting heat at my back as we moved through the suite. The master bathroom was every bit as luxurious as the rest of the penthouse—marble floors, a massive glass shower with multiple jets, and soft lighting that created an intimate, almost dreamlike atmosphere.

I started the water, letting it run hot before stepping into the spacious shower. Gage was right behind me, the door closing us off from the rest of the world. The second the water hit my skin, I sighed, feeling the tension of the day began to melt away.

But the relief was short-lived as Gage pressed up against me, his body firm and demanding. His hands found my hips, pulling me back against his chest, and I could feel every inch of him, hard and ready. The steam rose around us, cocooning us in our own little world as his lips found the curve of my neck, his teeth grazing the sensitive skin.

"Damn, you feel good," he murmured against my skin, his hands sliding up to cup my breasts, his thumbs brushing over my nipples. The heat from the water was nothing compared to the heat of his touch, and I arched into him, a soft moan slipping from my lips.

We moved together, our bodies slick and wet under the cascade of water as we washed each other. His hands were everywhere as he cleaned me, exploring, teasing, and driving me crazy with need. But he didn't push too far, didn't take it all the way. Instead, he kept me on the edge, his mouth and hands working in tandem to keep the tension simmering just below the surface.

I turned in his arms, my hands sliding up his chest, feeling the hard muscle beneath my fingers. I looked up at him, my heart pounding in my chest, and saw the desire burning in his eyes, mirrored by the flames licking at my insides.

"I'm so proud of you, baby. This was my first fight in Vegas, and I was front row. Watching my man up there land punches like it's easy had my nipples tingling. And when you won and held up that championship belt...I might have creamed my panties a little bit. And right now, you got me all kinds of turned-on, handsome. I can't say enough how proud I am of you. Let me show you," I whispered, dropping my hand down to wrap around his thick length. "And you were so good while you were training, sticking to celibacy. But now that you've won the fight, you deserve a reward."

His breath hitched as he watched me sink to my knees, the water cascading over us, making everything glisten and shine. I looked up at him, holding his gaze as I leaned in and took him into my mouth.

The groan that rumbled through his chest was deep and primal, and it sent a shiver down my spine. I kept my pace slow at first, teasing him with the flick of my tongue and the gentle suction of my lips. But as his hands tangled in my hair, guiding my movements, I picked up the pace, taking him deeper, harder, wanting to make this good for him —no, great for him.

The sound of the water, the slickness of his dick in my mouth, the way he whispered my name— every part of it was intoxicating. I could feel his body tensing, his thighs trembling as he fought to keep control, but I wasn't going to let him. Not tonight. I wanted to push him over the edge, to make him feel the way he'd made me feel so many times before.

I hollowed my cheeks, sucking him deeper, my hand working the base as I bobbed my head, my tongue swirling around the tip each time I pulled back. His breathing grew ragged, his hands gripping my hair tighter as he fucked my mouth, his hips bucking in time with my movements.

"Vanessa, shit..." His voice was strained, a warning, but I didn't let up. I wanted to taste him, wanted to feel him lose control. I sucked him harder, taking him as deep as I could until his body went rigid, his groans echoing off the tile walls as he came, hot and thick, down my throat.

I swallowed every drop, savoring the taste of him, the way his body shuddered with each wave of pleasure. When he finally released my hair, I pulled back, looking up at him, a satisfied smile tugging at my lips.

He stared down at me, his chest heaving, his eyes dark with lust and something else—something deeper. He reached down, pulling me up to my feet, and captured my lips in a searing kiss, his hands roaming over my body, his touch possessive, claiming. "Damn, girl," he whispered against my lips. "That mouth - just lethal, in and out of the bedroom."

I smiled, feeling a surge of pride at the way I'd made him feel. "Duh," I said cheekily.

Gage shook his head, then bent his neck, bringing his mouth back to mine. He kissed me, slower this time, more tender, his hands cradling my face as if I were something precious. And at that moment, with the water still streaming over us, everything felt right.

We finally stepped out of the shower, and I could tell by the glint in his eyes that the night was far from over. I wasn't sure what Gage had planned next, but I was ready to find out. I trusted him completely, and whatever he had in mind, I knew I wanted to do it.

The move from the steamy shower to the spacious master bedroom felt seamless, almost like stepping into another world—one where the only thing that existed was Gage and the promise of what was to come. The suite was bathed in a soft, ambient glow, the lighting low enough to create shadows that danced along the walls. It was the perfect backdrop for whatever Gage had planned next.

As we toweled each other off, Gage's touch was uncharacteristically gentle, a stark contrast to the fire that had been simmering between us just moments ago. His hands lingered on my skin, each stroke deliberate, almost reverent. It sent a shiver down my spine, and I found myself wondering what he was thinking. His eyes were dark and intense, as if he was holding something back.

Once we were both dry, Gage took my hand and led me to the bed, the anticipation building with every step. The bed was massive, draped in soft, luxurious sheets that beckoned us to lose ourselves in them. Gage motioned for me to lie down, and I did so willingly, the cool fabric beneath me contrasting with the warmth still radiating from my skin.

Gage stepped back, his gaze sweeping over my body, his expression thoughtful, almost contemplative. I bit my lip, waiting, my heart pounding in my chest.

"I wanna try something," Gage said, his voice a low rumble that sent a thrill of excitement through me. He reached into the nightstand drawer and pulled out a silk tie. The sight of it sent my pulse racing, my body instinctively reacting to the idea of what was about to happen.

"You trust me?" he asked, his tone softening as he sat on the edge of the bed, the tie dangling from his fingers.

"With my life," I whispered back, my voice barely audible over the sound of my own heartbeat.

Gage's smile was slight but genuine as he leaned in, his lips brushing mine in a featherlight kiss. Then, he slowly slipped the tie over my eyes, the darkness enveloping me as the world faded away, leaving only the sensation of his hands on me.

"Lie back," he instructed, and I obeyed, the anticipation bubbling up inside me like a heady mixture of nerves and excitement.

The first touch of warm oil on my skin was like a jolt of electricity, igniting every nerve ending in my body. Gage's hands were strong yet gentle, gliding over my shoulders, down my arms, across my chest, and lower. Each stroke was purposeful, his fingers kneading the tension from my muscles while simultaneously building the tension inside me.

His voice was a low murmur in my ear, a mix of dirty, sweet nothings that made me blush even as I ached for more. He knew exactly what he was doing, how to push my buttons, how to keep me on the edge of pleasure without tipping me over. It was intoxicating, losing myself in the feel of his hands, in the sound of his voice.

As he worked his way down my body, the pressure of his hands shifted from firm to featherlight, teasing, tantalizing. My breath hitched as he slid his hands down my thighs, spreading the oil over every inch of my skin. I felt like I was floating, every part of me focused on his touch, the world outside of us completely forgotten.

But then, something changed.

It was subtle at first—just a slight difference in the way his hands moved, a difference in the pressure, in the rhythm. I frowned, trying to process the shift through the haze of pleasure clouding my mind. The hands on my body felt different, a little rougher, familiar, but definitely not the same hands that had been rubbing me down. Or was I so clouded with pleasure and lust that I was imagining it? Confusion flickered through me, breaking through the fog.

"Gage?" I called out, expecting his voice to come from right beside me, where I'd last heard him.

Instead, his reply came from across the room. "I'm right here, baby," he said, his voice calm, steady.

Panic shot through me, cold and sharp, cutting through the warmth of the massage. My hands flew up to the blindfold, desperate to pull it off, to see what the hell was going on. My heart was pounding in my chest, the tension in my body no longer the pleasurable kind.

But before I could yank the tie away, a hand—a different hand—gently caught my wrist, stopping me.

"It's okay, love. It's Vince. You're okay."

My breath caught in my throat, my mind racing. Vince? Here? I couldn't make sense of it, couldn't process what he was saying, what was happening. My heart was still pounding, the confusion making my head spin.

I could feel the bedspread gently cover my naked body as the blindfold was loosened, and the world slowly came back into focus as the soft light of the room flooded my vision. My eyes darted to the side, finding Vince kneeling beside me, his expression calm and reassuring. Gage was standing at the foot of the bed, watching me with an unreadable look in his eyes.

"What... I don't... I don't understand," I stammered, my voice shaky as I looked between the two of them.

Gage stepped forward, his gaze softening as he reached out, brushing a hand down my arm. "I know this is... unexpected - crazy even," he began, his voice carrying a deep sincerity that made my breath catch. "But we had to do something. Things have been so tense, so tight since we stepped off that plane."

He paused, his fingers tracing light, soothing patterns on my skin as if trying to ground me in the moment. "Vanessa, sweetheart, I've seen how you've been trying to hold it together, how you've been carrying all this anxiety. I can see it in your eyes every time you look at me, every time you glance over at Vince. It's like you're caught in this impossible situation, torn between two parts of yourself. It hurts me to see you like that."

Gage's voice grew softer, more vulnerable, as he continued. "I care about you more than I can put into words. All I want is to make you happy, to give you what you need. And I'm not blind. I can see that being with me—and only me—isn't enough. And I don't say that in a bad way. It's just... I see the way you look at Vince - the way you try to hide it, but I see it, and I can't ignore it. And I thought about what to do. Being done with you wasn't an option. You're too much a part of me. You're in my fucking blood, V. So, I realized... maybe what you need isn't just one of us. Maybe it's both of us. Maybe that's what will truly make you happy."

His eyes searched mine, seeking understanding, acceptance. "I'm not saying this is going to be easy or that I have all the answers, but I know that I can't stand the thought of you feeling torn. And after how things went down this weekend... I'm sure you feel like you have to make a decision, a choice. But you don't. Not when there's another way, a way for you to have everything you want, everything you need."

Gage's hand slipped from my arm to cup my cheek, his thumb brushing away a tear I hadn't realized had fallen. "This isn't just about me or Vince. This is about you, V. About what you need - what you deserve. And that's to be loved fully, completely, without having to sacrifice a part of yourself. That's why we're doing this—why we're both here. We wanna give you that because we care about you too much to do anything else."

His words resonated deep within me, shaking loose the fear and confusion that had been clinging to my heart. The idea that I didn't have to choose, that I could have them both, that I could be with them both—was that really possible? Could something this beautiful, this unexpected, actually work?

Gage leaned in, pressing a gentle kiss to my forehead, a gesture so tender it made my heart ache. "We're here for you, V, the both of us. All that matters is that you're protected and happy."

CHAPTER TWENTY

VANESSA

The air in the master bedroom was thick with anticipation, the atmosphere crackling with a mixture of desire, tension, and something deeper —something that spoke of love, trust, and the breaking of boundaries. I sat in the middle of the bed, my heart pounding in my chest, trying to make sense of the whirlwind of emotions coursing through me.

Vince and Gage stood before me, both of them watching me with eyes that burned with intent. There was no jealousy between them, no tension —just a shared purpose, a shared desire to give me everything I needed, everything I wanted. The realization that I didn't have to choose between them - that I could have them both, had settled deep within me, and a warmth spread through my entire being.

Vince leaned down and placed his fisted hands on either side of me on the bed, caging me in. His expression was serious but tender. "Vanessa, love," he began, his voice low, almost hesitant. "This... this whole thing is not something I thought I would ever be faced with. But here I am... and I want you just as much now as I did before we got to Vegas. Seeing you with Vince didn't change that. I need you to know that. I need you to understand that I wouldn't be here, doing this, if I didn't care about you. Honestly, you're it for me. So, if this is how I can have you, so be it."

He paused, his gaze holding mine, searching for understanding. "When Gage and I talked last night, it wasn't just about making this work between us three. It was about figuring out what was best. We knew where we stood. There's no animosity or jealousy here. We understand that what we have with you is our own. What you share with Vince has nothing to do with me or vice versa. But it was important to make sure it was something you'd be happy with. Because, V, you deserve to be happy, to be loved fully, and if this is what it takes to make that happen, then I'm all in. I want you to know that you're not just getting Gage and Vince. I think I speak for both of us when I say you're getting all of us—our love, our support, everything we have to offer."

I felt tears prick at the corners of my eyes, overwhelmed by the sincerity in his voice and the depth of his feelings. Vince had always been steady and reliable, but seeing him open up like this, seeing him lay his emotions bare, was something else entirely. It made my heart swell with affection, with gratitude, with love.

"Vince..." I whispered, my voice shaky as I reached out to touch his hand. "I don't... I don't even know what to say." I looked over at Gage. "And you." My gaze swung back to Vince. "You both are just... just so amazing. The way you care for me - put me first, it's just... thank you. I-I love you both. I want you both."

The smile that lit my men's faces was everything. My heart was so full, it nearly burst out of my chest.

Gage stepped closer then, his hand brushing against mine as he leaned in, his lips finding the curve of my neck. "So, now that we are officially a trio, I say we seal the union in the most pleasurable way possible," he murmured, his voice a low rumble that sent shivers down my spine.

"Absolutely," I breathed, my entire body vibrating with anticipation, with need.

The tension in the room shifted then, from emotional to physical, the air thickening with desire. Vince's hand slid up my arm, his touch firm yet gentle, while Gage's lips trailed down to my collarbone, his breath warm against my skin. I closed my eyes, losing myself in the sensations, in the feel of their hands on me, their mouths exploring every inch of my body.

A rush of anticipation surged through me, mixing with a sense of nervous excitement. This was uncharted territory—a boundary I had never crossed before. The reality of what was about to happen sent a shiver down my spine. I was about to have my first threesome, a moment that felt both thrilling and terrifying all at once. But in that moment, as I sat between my two loves, the fear faded, replaced by a profound sense of trust.

There were no two other men I'd rather share this level of intimacy with. Gage and Vince—both strong, both protective, both loving in their own distinct ways—were the only ones I could ever imagine opening myself up to like this. It wasn't just about physical pleasure; it was about the connection we shared, the deep emotional bonds that had been forged over time.

My heart raced, and a soft moan escaped my lips as Vince's hand traced the curve of my waist, his touch steadying me, grounding me. Gage's lips continued their descent, each kiss setting my skin ablaze with need. The room seemed to close in around us, the outside world falling away until it was just the three of us, locked in this moment of intense, shared intimacy.

I was already naked, but my fellas were still partially clothed, and that wasn't going to do. I wanted them just as bare, just as exposed as I was. I climbed off the bed, and the comforter slid away from my body, revealing all my naked glory. Slowly, deliberately, I reached for Vince's shirt, my fingers curling around the hem as I tugged it upward, revealing the hard planes of his chest. He raised his arms, letting me pull the fabric over his head before tossing it aside.

My hands roamed over his chest, tracing the lines of his muscles, feeling the heat of his skin under my palms. Gage stood behind me, his mouth against my neck, his eyes dark with hunger.

I took my time, savoring every moment, every touch, every look that passed between us. Vince's joggers were next, the fabric sliding easily down his legs as I knelt before him, my eyes never leaving his as I helped him step out of them.

When he was finally naked, I leaned in, pressing a soft kiss to his stomach, my hands gliding up his thighs. Vince groaned softly, his hand tangling in my hair as he pulled me back up, his lips capturing mine in a deep, hungry kiss.

But I wasn't done yet.

I turned to Gage, who was already shirtless, his chest heaving with barely contained desire. His basketball shorts hung low on his hips, and I made quick work of them, my fingers hooking into the waistband and pulling them down, revealing the rest of his sculpted body. He kicked them off, and I took a moment to admire the sight of him, of both of them, standing before me, ready, willing, and eager to make this night unforgettable.

Vince moved behind me, his hands sliding up my sides as he pressed his body against mine, his lips finding the sensitive spot just below my ear. Gage stepped closer, his hand cupping my cheek as he leaned in to kiss me, his tongue sliding against mine in a sensual dance that made my knees weak.

The world outside ceased to exist. It was just the three of us, wrapped up in each other, our bodies moving together in a rhythm that felt both new and familiar. Vince's hands roamed over my body, his touch sending sparks of pleasure through me, while Gage's kisses trailed down my neck, his teeth grazing my skin in a way that made me shiver with anticipation.

I gasped as Vince's lips found my throat, his teeth gently nipping at the tender flesh there. I swayed slightly, caught off balance as the dual sensations of their bodies pressing against mine, of their touches stoking the fire within me, threatened to overwhelm me. But they held me up, their hands on my body a steadying force in the midst of this whirlwind of desire.

Gage's strong fingers traced the curve of my breasts, his thumbs teasing my nipples until they hardened into sensitive peaks. Vince mirrored his movements on my back, his hands skimming down to cup my buttocks, squeezing gently as he pressed himself closer against me. I let out a whimper of need at the contact, my head falling back onto Vince's shoulder.

Vince's lips found my neck again, nibbling and sucking in a way that made every nerve ending in my body tingle with anticipation. Gage watched us for a moment before he joined, his lips moving lower to capture a nipple while one hand found its way between my legs. A gasp escaped me as I felt the first touch of his fingers against my soaked center. He stroked me gently, teasingly, before sliding a finger inside. A moan reverberated in my throat, my body arching into his touch as desire sparked through me.

This was uncharted territory for all of us but we moved together like clockwork, every touch, every caress perfectly in sync. Vince's hands were on my waist now, holding me steady as Gage explored me with his fingers. I could hear their breaths becoming heavier, matching the rhythm of my own heart, which beat wildly against my chest.

I reached behind me, seeking Vince's hardness, and he obliged without hesitation, sighing into my ear as I touched him. At the same time, Gage's mouth left my breast to capture my lips in a searing kiss. His tongue danced with mine, mimicking the movements his fingers made inside me.

Vince gripped my waist and pulled us back towards the bed. His eager hands moved to the front, capturing my breasts. He kneaded them tenderly, his thumbs circling my nipples, making them rock hard.

"Lay down, love," Vince whispered in my ear.

I quickly obliged, detangling myself from Gage and falling backward onto the soft sheets. I pulled Gage with me. He hovered above me as Vince circled around us to the edge of the bed. I watched, breathless, as Vince moved to the foot of the bed, his dark eyes never leaving our entangled bodies. I could feel the heat of their gazes on me, igniting a fire deep within.

Gage's lips found mine again, his kisses gentle and demanding at the same time. One of his hands was still tangled in my hair, holding me still as he deepened the kiss. His other hand continued its journey, tracing a path down my body until it reached my center again. His fingers dipped inside, teasing me with slow strokes that matched the rhythm of his tongue against mine.

Breaking our kiss, Gage moved lower, leaving a trail of hot kisses along my neck and chest until he reached my breasts again. He took a nipple into his mouth, sucking gently as his fingers continued their stimulating exploration between my thighs.

Meanwhile, Vince had positioned himself between my spread legs. He ran his hands up and down my inner thighs before he replaced Gage's fingers with his mouth.

A gasp slipped from my mouth as Vince started working his tongue against my sensitive flesh. His hands held my thighs apart, preventing me from squirming as the sensations overwhelmed me. Gage took that moment to pull away too, sitting back on his heels and stroking himself while watching Vince driving me crazy with his mouth.

"Touch that kitty for me, V," Gage whispered, his gaze heated and intense. I complied without hesitation, my hand moving down to touch myself. The combination of Vince's tongue and my own fingers quickly pushed me closer to the edge. My hips bucked against Vince's face, and he gripped me tighter, redoubling his efforts and making me moan louder.

Just when I thought I couldn't take any more pleasure, Gage moved back in, replacing my hand with his own. He matched Vince's rhythm, their movements perfectly synchronized to drive me over the edge.

My climax hit me like a bolt of lightning, pleasure rippling through every part of my body in wave after wave of pure, undeniable ecstasy. My body quivered, and I cried out, my sounds of pleasure echoing throughout the room. Vince didn't stop his ministrations, his tongue continuing to work me through my climax until the sensations were almost too much to bear.

Finally, they gave me a moment to breathe, their hands and mouths leaving me flushed and panting as I lay sprawled on the bed. I was spent but not sated; our night was far from over.

I could feel the sheets beneath me, still warm from our previous entanglements, as Gage gently guided me to turn over onto my hands and knees. His firm hand pressed against my backside, deepening the arch in my back before he gripped my cheeks, giving them a good squeeze before parting them and slamming his thick, veiny dick deep inside me. A surprised gasp pulled from my throat at the sensation - a balance of discomfort and pleasure. His rough fingers dug into my hips as he pounded into me.

Vince remained at the foot of the bed, his eyes watching us hungrily in the dim light. He was still wearing that enigmatic smile, his fingers lazily stroking his length. After a minute, he moved closer, placing himself before me with an invitation in his eyes. I accepted willingly, taking him into my mouth. I closed my eyes around him while concentrating on matching Gage's rhythmic thrusts.

Gage was relentless, his hands guiding my hips back onto him mercilessly as he filled me repeatedly. His breath was heavy and ragged in my ear, his grip on my hips tightening with each powerful thrust. I gripped Vince harder, taking him deeper into my mouth as my own pleasure mounted.

Suddenly, I felt Vince's fingers gently tangle in my hair, guiding my rhythm onto him. With Gage inside me and Vince in my mouth, I was lost to the sensory overload. My moans were muffled around Vince, heightening the erotic charge filling the room.

Gage pulled back slightly, the head of his dick teasing at my entrance before he slammed home again. The change in angle hit a new spot deep within me, making me cry out in pleasure. Vince's grip on my hair tightened in response as he bucked his hips, driving himself deeper into my welcoming mouth.

I was completely at their mercy, sandwiched between two men who knew exactly how to push each and every one of my buttons. Their grunts and groans filled the room, mixing with my own pleasure-filled whimpers and cries. My body was a conduit of their lust, burning hot and trembling with desire.

Gage's thrusts became even more relentless, striking against my core with a rhythm that was as intoxicating as it was tortuously slow. Each powerful drive in drew a gasp from me, which was promptly silenced by Vince as he deepened his presence in my mouth.

My body was a whirlwind of sensation: the pressure of Gage deep within me, the taste of Vince on my tongue, the friction against my sensitive skin. But more than that, I felt desired, cherished even, by these two incredible men who were devoting their attention to my pleasure.

Vince moved a hand down to caress my breasts, his thumb flicking over an already hard nipple. I moaned in response, taking him even deeper into my mouth. His grip on my hair tightened, and I knew he was close.

Gage's pace quickened at the same time. He drove into me so hard the bed shook underneath us. His hand snaked around to tease my clit, his fingers moving in time with his thrusts.

Vince's fingers pressed harder into my scalp, and he thrust up into my mouth once, twice, before I felt him shudder. Hot jets of pleasure filled my mouth as he came, his breath catching in a long moan that echoed through the room.

The sight and taste of Vince's climax pushed me even closer to the edge. My body clenched around Gage's dick, squeezing him tightly with every pulse of Vince's release. He groaned behind me, his thrusts becoming more erratic as he, too, approached his climax.

When it finally hit, it was like a dam had broken inside me. Pleasure swept through me in wave after wave, washing over every nerve ending and leaving me trembling in its wake. I screamed around Vince in my mouth, the combination of sounds making him twitch with sensitivity. Gage was still thrusting into me hard, prolonging my orgasm as he sought his own release.

With one last powerful thrust, he came with a deep groan that vibrated against my skin. His seed filled me, marking me as his, just as Vince had done when he filled my mouth and throat with his cum. Gage collapsed onto my back, his weight a comforting presence as we both trembled from the aftershocks of our orgasms.

Pulling out of me slowly, Gage gently turned me around to lay on my back. He fell onto the space next to me, both of us panting and sweaty from our exertions. Vince came through with a wet washcloth and cleaned me up before sliding behind me, sandwiching me between their hot bodies. I was enveloped in a cocoon of masculine scents: leather, musk, and something uniquely them.

The room was quiet now, the only sounds being our collective breathing slowly returning to normal and the soft hum of the air conditioning. The warmth of the moment still hung heavy in the air, wrapping us in a blanket of contentment and peace. I was nestled between Vince and Gage, our bodies tangled together in a way that felt natural, like this was how it was always meant to be.

Vince's arm was draped across my waist, his chest pressed against my back, while Gage's hand rested possessively on my thigh, his body curled protectively around me. It was as if they were each holding a piece of me, grounding me in this new reality we had created together.

For a long time, none of us spoke, content to simply be in the moment. I could feel the steady rise and fall of Vince's chest behind me, his heartbeat strong and reassuring against my back. Gage's breath was warm against my neck, a comforting presence that made me feel safe and cherished.

I let out a soft sigh, my fingers absentmindedly tracing patterns on Gage's chest as I stared up at the ceiling, my mind a whirl of thoughts and emotions. The reality of what had just happened was still sinking in, and with it came a profound sense of peace, of rightness. I had been worried, anxious even, about how this would all play out—about what it would mean for the three of us. But now, lying here between these two men who had shown me nothing but love and understanding, I realized that all those worries had been for nothing.

This wasn't just about the physical act of making love; it was about the emotional connection we shared, the bond that had been forged through trust and respect. It was about acceptance—accepting that it was okay to want them both, to need them both. And most importantly, it was about love—about the love we had for each other and the understanding that love didn't have to fit into neat, conventional boxes.

Gage shifted beside me, his fingers brushing a stray lock of hair from my face as he looked down at me, his expression soft, tender. "You good?" he asked, his voice low and filled with concern.

I turned my head to meet his gaze, a small smile playing on my lips. "Yeah," I replied, my voice barely above a whisper. "I'm more than good."

Vince's hand tightened slightly on my waist, a silent affirmation that he was there, that he was part of this too. I tilted my head back to look at him, my heart swelling with affection for this man who was my rock, my steady anchor in the storm.

"You were amazing," Vince said, his voice rumbling in his chest as he spoke. "Both of you," he added cheekily.

Gage chuckled softly, his hand squeezing my thigh in agreement. "You know what they say about teamwork..."

I giggled. "Ya'll are wild."

"Wild about you," Gage countered and a I felt a warmth spread through me at his words. At the realization that we were in this together, all three of us, and that knowledge brought with it a sense of security, of belonging. And I knew, without a doubt, that whatever the future held, we would face it together—stronger, more connected, and more in love than ever before.

EPILOGUE

Months Later

VINCE

I awoke to soft, rhythmic moaning filling the room, blending perfectly with the early morning light filtering through the curtains. I blinked slowly, my mind still clouded with sleep, but the sound—Vanessa's unmistakable moans of pleasure —had me fully awake in seconds.

I didn't move at first, not wanting to disrupt the beautiful sight that greeted me. Gage was sprawled beneath Vanessa, his hands gripping her waist as she rode him like a woman possessed. Her head was thrown back, her eyes squeezed shut, lost in the throes of passion. The way her body moved, fluid and uninhibited, was like watching a symphony unfold—a sensual, mesmerizing performance that I'd come to treasure.

This was my new normal, I realized, waking up to the sight of the woman I loved entwined with another man who loved her just as much as I did. It was unconventional, yes, but it worked for us—for the three of us. And for the first time in a long time, I felt a deep sense of peace, like I was exactly where

I was supposed to be.

I watched as Vanessa's movements became more frantic, her hips circling with increasing urgency. Her breathing was ragged, each exhale accompanied by a soft cry that sent a thrill of excitement through my veins. Gage's hands tightened on her waist, his body tensing beneath her as he thrust upward to meet her rhythm.

I knew our girl was close, teetering on the edge of release, and I couldn't resist adding to her pleasure. I reached out, my fingers brushing against her flushed skin before finding her nipple, rolling it between my fingers and pinching it just hard enough to send a shock of pleasure through her.

Vanessa cried out, her entire body shuddering as the orgasm tore through her. The sight of her coming undone was beautiful, a raw display of the passion and love we all shared. I couldn't help but smile, satisfied that I had contributed to her pleasure, even if I hadn't been the one inside her.

Gage groaned beneath her, his own release following quickly behind, and they collapsed together in a tangle of limbs, breathing heavily as the aftershocks of their orgasms slowly faded.

I watched them for a moment longer, content to let them have their moment before I slipped out of bed and headed to the bathroom. I turned on the shower, letting the steam fill the room as I stepped under the spray, the hot water soothing my muscles. I couldn't help but smile, thinking about how much things had changed—how much I had changed. It wasn't something I ever expected, sharing the woman I loved with another man, but here we were. And, strangely, it worked.

I was just starting to soap up when I heard the bathroom door open. I didn't need to turn around to know who it was. Vanessa's presence filled the space, her energy unmistakable. I felt her move closer, the heat of her body radiating against my back before her arms slipped around my waist, her hands roaming over my abs and lower until she found what she was looking for.

"Morning," she purred, her voice still thick with the remnants of sleep and pleasure.

"Morning," I murmured back, my voice deeper than usual, roughened by sleep and desire. My body responded to her instantly, hardening under her touch.

Vanessa didn't waste any time. She dropped to her knees, her hands gripping my hips as she took me into her mouth. Fuck, she knew exactly what she was doing—how to drive me crazy in all the best ways. I let out a low groan, my hands finding their way into her hair and gripping the curly bun she'd pulled it into on top of her head, guiding her movements as she worked her magic. My stomach tightened, and my toes curled as she sucked me in deep and hollowed out her cheeks.

The sensation was pure bliss, a tight coil of ecstasy winding up inside me under Vanessa's expert ministrations. "Fuck, Vanessa..." I muttered through gritted teeth, my muscles tensing as the pleasure mounted. A smug giggle left her lips, the vibration around my throbbing length pushing me closer to the edge. I pulled out, not wanting to come yet. I wanted to feel her hot pussy pulling and squeezing my shit.

I gently pulled her to her feet. "Turn around," I whispered against her ear, my voice rough with want.

She did as I asked, her movements slow, deliberate. I pressed her against the cool tile, positioning myself behind her. I hooked one of her legs over my arm, and with one smooth thrust, I was inside her, and it was everything I needed. Everything I wanted.

The water streamed over us as I set a hard, fast pace, my hands gripping her hips, pulling her back onto me as I pounded into her. Her moans echoed in the shower, bouncing off the tiles and mixing with the sounds of our bodies colliding. She felt so fucking good. So tight and wet, as she squeezed me perfectly with every movement.

I buried my face in her neck, inhaling her scent —soap, sweat, and something uniquely Vanessa. I could feel her trembling, her body responding to mine, and it was driving me crazy.

"I can feel you, V," I growled against her ear, tightening my grip on her hips. "I can feel how close you are."

"Y-yes, baby. I'm s-so fucking close," she gasped, her voice barely a whisper.

That was all it took. I lost myself in her, in the way she felt, the way she sounded, the way she tasted as I pressed my lips to her neck, marking her as mine even as I shared her with Gage.

She cried out, her body shaking with the force of her orgasm, and I followed her over the edge, my release hitting me with the intensity of a freight train. We collapsed together, spent and satisfied, the water washing away the evidence of our morning tryst.

When we finally pulled apart, she turned to me, a lazy smile playing on her lips. "We should hurry and get ready," she said, her voice still breathless. "We have a wedding to get to."

I chuckled, leaning down to kiss her one last time. "Yeah, I guess we should."

With a final kiss, we stepped out of the shower to get ready for Gabby and Griff's big day.

VANESSA

The gentle hum of the car's engine was comforting background noise as I nestled between Vince and Gage, their warmth surrounding me, their presence a constant reassurance. The ride to the wedding venue was smooth, and as we glided through the streets of Eastbrook, I couldn't help but reflect on how much my life had changed since that unforgettable weekend in Vegas.

I had always thought I had a handle on things —a flourishing career, an unbreakable bond with Gabby, and a love life that, while complicated, was nothing I couldn't manage. But everything had shifted that weekend. The night Vince and Gage surprised me in the suite by professing their commitment to me, to us. The love that had blossomed between the three of us, though unconventional, was undeniable. It was as if I had been walking through life partially asleep, and now, having Vince and Gage openly by my side, I felt awake - alive in a way I never had before.

I glanced at Vince to my left, his hand resting protectively on my thigh, his thumb gently stroking my skin in lazy circles. He caught me looking at him and gave me a small, knowing smile that made my heart swell. On my right, Gage's arm was draped casually across the back of the seat, his fingers playing with the ends of my hair. He was humming softly, a contented expression on his face as he gazed out the window.

I closed my eyes for a moment, letting myself fully absorb the love and security I felt with them. This was my life now—a relationship that defied societal norms. One that challenged everything I thought I knew about love, but one that felt more right than anything I'd ever experienced. I was happy, content, and deeply in love with both of them. And the best part? They were just as deeply in love with me.

As the car pulled up to the wedding venue, I felt a rush of excitement. Today wasn't just a big day for Gabby and Griff; it was a celebration of love, of friendship, of everything we held dear. And I was ready to soak in every moment of it.

We stepped out of the car, and Gage leaned in to kiss my cheek before heading off to join Griff and the other groomsmen. Vince squeezed my hand, his touch lingering before he, too, made his way inside to enjoy some pre-wedding light bites and cocktails. I watched them go, my heart swelling with affection before I turned and headed inside to find Gabby and Momma Gwen in the bridal suite.

The suite was a whirlwind of activity when I walked in. Gabby was sitting in a plush chair in front of a large mirror, her hair in the process of being expertly curled while she chatted animatedly with Momma Gwen. The room was filled with the scent of flowers and the sound of laughter, a joyful buzz that filled me with warmth.

"Hey, maid of honor!" Gabby called out when she saw me, her eyes lighting up with excitement. "Come on, V! Sit down; we've got to get you all glammed up!"

I grinned and made my way over to her, giving her a quick hug before sitting down in the chair next to hers. Momma Gwen came over and kissed my cheek, her smile as warm and comforting as always.

"You girls are already so beautiful, but by the time these lovely stylists finish all this plucking and primping, y'all coochies gonna be fighting for their lives tonight. Trust," she said with a wink.

I burst out laughing, almost doubling over while Gabby's jaw fell open as she stared at Momma Gwen in disbelief.

"I swear, old woman, that mouth of yours gets wilder and wilder every day," Gabby lovingly chastised, but Momma Gwen just waved her off.

"Whatever. I already know Vanessa's cooch is already getting that good-good, the way she stumbled into this suite. I know them boys had you spread six ways from Sunday this morning," she ended with a chuckle.

"Momma Gwen!" I shouted as laughter overtook me. She was such a mess.

She just smirked and shrugged as she took the seat on the other side of Gabby.

As I sat for hair and makeup, I felt a deep sense of contentment settle over me. This was it—this was the life I had always wanted. Surrounded by the people I loved, about to watch my best friend marry the man of her dreams. And to top it all off, I had my own two loves waiting for me just outside.

While the stylist worked her magic, I found myself catching Gabby's gaze in the mirror. Her smile softened, and for a moment, it was just the two of us sharing a silent understanding. We'd been through so much together, and here we were, on the cusp of the next chapter in our lives.

"I'm so proud of you, Gabby," I said softly, my voice thick with emotion. "You're gonna be the most beautiful bride."

Gabby's eyes shimmered with tears, but her smile didn't waver. "Thank you, V. I wouldn't be here without you. You've always been my rock."

"Right back at you," I whispered, my heart full.

As we finished getting ready, the room buzzed with excitement. We helped Gabby into her gown, the dress a stunning masterpiece of lace and satin that hugged her curves perfectly. She looked breathtaking, and when Momma Gwen started to cry, it was the final seal of approval.

Before we knew it, it was time to head out. The ceremony was set to take place in the garden, under a canopy of flowers that looked like something out of a fairytale. As we walked out to take our places, I took a deep breath, letting the beauty of the scene wash over me.

Gabby and Griff's wedding was everything I imagined it would be. The vows they exchanged were full of love and promise, each word a testament to the bond they shared. Standing beside Gabby as she pledged her life to Griff, I couldn't help but feel a surge of joy for her—for both of them.

As they kissed to seal their vows, I found myself glancing over at Vince, who was sitting in the second row, and Gage, who was standing next to Griff as his best man. My heart skipped a beat as I thought about us—about what our future might look like. I couldn't help but wonder if, one day, we might have our own version of a commitment ceremony, a way to celebrate the unique and powerful love we shared.

For now, though, I was content. Content to be here, to be part of this beautiful day, and to be loved by two incredible men who made me feel like the luckiest woman in the world.

As the ceremony ended and we made our way back down the aisle, I couldn't help but smile.

Everything was perfect. Absolutely perfect.

GAGE

The reception was in full swing, the room buzzing with energy as people danced, laughed, and celebrated Gabby and Griff's love. The music pulsed through the air, a steady beat that seemed to vibrate in my chest as I stood at the edge of the dance floor, watching the scene unfold.

I wasn't much of a dancer—never had been—but that didn't stop me from appreciating the way Vanessa moved. She was out there, lost in the music, her laughter bright and infectious as she spun around with Gabby. The two of them were a sight to behold, all smiles and joy, their bond palpable even from where I stood.

Vanessa looked radiant, absolutely glowing with happiness. Her dress clung to her in all the right places, the soft fabric swirling around her legs as she danced. Her hair was loose, cascading down her back in waves that shimmered in the soft lighting. But it was her smile that really got to me—wide and genuine, lighting up her entire face. She was beautiful, inside and out, and I felt a surge of love so strong it nearly knocked the breath out of me.

I couldn't take my eyes off her. Everything about her captivated me—the way she moved, the way she laughed, the way she threw her head back in pure, unadulterated joy. I loved her. Fuck, I loved her more than I'd ever thought possible.

The way she was with Gabby, the ease with which she moved through the world, the strength she had to embrace this unconventional relationship—it all made me love her even more. She was perfect for me, for Vince, for the life we were building together. And as I stood there, watching her, I felt like the luckiest man alive.

It hadn't always been easy. Hell, there were days when I questioned how we were going to make this work—how the hell three people could navigate a relationship without it all falling apart. But Vanessa made it easy. She made everything feel right. Being with her and building a close bond with Vince, it was like we'd all found something we hadn't even known we were looking for. Something that completed us in a way we never expected.

I watched as she spun Gabby around one last time, both of them laughing so hard they could barely keep their balance. When the song ended, they collapsed against each other, still giggling, and I knew it was my moment.

I pushed away from the bar and made my way over to them, my eyes locked on Vanessa. She caught sight of me approaching, and her smile softened into something more intimate, more personal. My heart skipped a beat as I reached them, and Gabby, bless her, winked at me before slipping away, leaving me alone with the love of my life.

"May I have this dance?" I asked, my voice low, but the smile on my face was all Vanessa needed to know how much I wanted this moment.

"Only if you promise not to step on my toes," she teased, her eyes sparkling with mischief.

"I'll do my best," I replied, pulling her into my arms. The moment she was in my grasp, everything else seemed to fade away. The music, the people, the noise—it all melted into the background until it was just the two of us, moving together as one.

We swayed to the music, our bodies pressed close, her warmth seeping into me as we moved in perfect sync. I rested my forehead against hers, our breaths mingling in the small space between us, and for a moment, I just held her, letting the feel of her in my arms ground me in a way nothing else could.

"You look absolutely stunning, V," I whispered, my lips brushing against her ear. "I haven't been able to take my eyes off you."

Vanessa blushed, her smile growing even softer as her eyes met mine, filled with a warmth that made my chest tighten with emotion. "You don't look so bad yourself, handsome," she whispered back, her voice laced with affection. "But you know, you never need to say anything to make me feel beautiful. I always feel like the most beautiful, most loved woman in the world when I'm with you."

Her words hit me straight in the heart, and for a moment, I couldn't find the right words. All I could do was hold her tighter, my hand sliding up her back to cradle the nape of her neck. This woman

—this incredible, strong, beautiful woman—had turned my world upside down, and I couldn't be more grateful.

"I never thought I'd be in a relationship like this," I confessed, my voice a bit gravellier than I intended. "But damn, V, it works. I don't care what anyone thinks. All that matters is you, me, Vince, and what we have. And you know what? I wouldn't change a thing."

Vanessa's eyes softened, a look of understanding and something deeper passing between us. "Gage," she started, her voice tender, "me either. You and Vince—what we have—it's special, it's real, and I wouldn't trade it for anything in the world."

Hearing her say that, feeling the sincerity in her words, made something inside me settle—like a puzzle piece clicking into place. All the doubts, all the questions about whether we could really make this work, faded away. What we had was real, and as long as we were honest with each other, as long as we stayed true to the love we shared, we could handle anything.

"I love you, Dimples," I said, my voice firm, leaving no room for doubt. "I love you, and I'll always be here for you. No matter what. You understand?"

Tears shimmered in her eyes, but she smiled, a smile so full of love it made my heart clench. "I understand, and I love you too, Gage," she whispered, her voice thick with emotion. "So much."

I leaned down and kissed her, slow and deep, pouring every ounce of love and gratitude I felt for her into that kiss. The world around us disappeared, leaving just the two of us in that moment, connected in a way that transcended words.

When we finally pulled back, Vanessa's cheeks were flushed, her lips slightly swollen from the kiss. But she looked happier than I'd ever seen her —radiant, glowing with the love we shared. And in that moment, I knew that no matter what challenges lay ahead, we'd face them together, stronger for the bond we'd forged.

THE END

AFTERWORD

Hey Rowdy's Rebels!

Yes, you! You finish any of my books and we crew. lol! You a Rowdy Rebel now!!

Real talk, thank you so much for taking the time to read this story. I hope you enjoyed Vanessa's journey as much as I loved writing it. Your support means everything to me. If Vanessa's story moved you in any way, please consider leaving a review. Your feedback helps other readers discover the book and allows me to keep creating the stories you love.

Alright! Enough of that. Let's keep in touch. Stay up to date on new releases and other content by following me on my socials or visiting my website.

Website: www.authorrowdyrooksy.com
Instagram: @authorrowdyrooksy
TikTok: @authorrowdyrooksy

BOOKS BY AUTHOR ROWDY ROOKSY

Contemporary Titles
Thorns And Gloves
Love And Legacy
The Assignment
One Weekend

Dark Academia
Dare: A Bradford Academy Novel (Book 1)

Kindle Vella Serial Drama
Blackwood

ABOUT THE AUTHOR

Rowdy Rooksy

Rowdy is a writer, filmmaker, traveler and occasional podcaster with a deep love for all things creative. By day, she deftly balances the corporate world as a Technical Project Manager and by  night she weaves spicy love stories with alpha males and strong FMCs.

While Texas is her home base, Rowdy's passion for travel means she's rarely there. On the off chance you do catch her in town, you'll probably find her binge-watching documentaries, reading dark spicy romance novels, or indulging in Haribo Gummy Bears.

www.ingramcontent.com/pod-product-compliance
Lightning Source LLC
Chambersburg PA
CBHW050338030726
47503CB00008B/2509